Altie — Search for the joy in life!

Seeker of
FORTUNE'S ANGEL

Carol J. Woodard

Carol J Woodard

Inspiring Voices®
A Service of **Guideposts**

Inspiring Voices books may be ordered through booksellers or by contacting:

Inspiring Voices
1663 Liberty Drive
Bloomington, IN 47403
www.inspiringvoices.com
1-(866) 697-5313

ISBN: 978-1-4624-0413-1 (e)
ISBN: 978-1-4624-0414-8 (sc)

Library of Congress Control Number: 2012922313

Printed in the United States of America

Inspiring Voices rev. date:11/28/2012

To my grandmother, for a strong faith
passed down through generations.
To my mother, for the vision to dream
and accomplish anything.
To my nephew, whose writing inspired me to write.
To Michael, who brought me renewed hope.
To my friends, who helped form my
desire to live life to the fullest.
To my recent friend, Mary, whose
encouragement kept my spirit soaring.

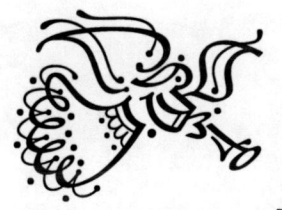

Part One

FAITH

CHAPTER 1

As I walked into the library, I instantly felt as though eyes were watching me. That thought wouldn't have occurred to me if I hadn't been carrying Shiloh in my bookbag. Why is it that the simple act of entering a public building with notices proclaiming no admittance to man's best friend can stir anxiety up in all of us? What on earth could be their reasoning for declaring the warmest of all animals off limits? Of course, I was certain the woman behind the huge oak desk would stop me in my tracks, and I was pleasantly surprised when I actually made it to the section marked *Travel* on the second floor.

Having extra time in my life was so new to me, and I was beginning to ask myself whether I had made the right decision. Working at the same job for over thirteen years—right out of college—gave me security, and I was surprised when they offered 150 of us three months' severance pay if we would simply walk away. After two months of looking for a job, I was starting to worry. As my head turned left and right, I could see only alphabetical names of countries begging me to stop before them. I walked slowly up and down each aisle. Suddenly, I heard a whimpering from the red bookbag I was carrying on my back. *Oh my gosh! How could I have forgotten the one thing I had taken so much time to hide (the thing that would mean expulsion from this noble structure if found)?* I immediately settled at a long table and brought Shiloh's hideaway onto my lap. "Shh, it's all right," I whispered as my hand touched his tiny head.

Looking around for any sign of life, I slowly brought out into the open the one gift I had been given that had been my guiding factor on whom to trust in my life's journey. This small apricot-colored ball of fluff had instincts far surpassing my own and had saved me more than once as I ventured in and out of my many relationships. He was my ever-constant companion.

My sweatshirt easily covered Shiloh's tiny body as I walked back and forth, hoping a book would jump out at me and beg for my attention. As

1

much confidence as I had in my little one's preference of boyfriends, he could not select which destination would land me this seemingly unbelievable job. I had considered not answering the oddly worded ad in the paper, but since I'd opted to take the voluntary severance package, this opportunity allowed me to at least envision myself as a successful thirty-something again. The task at hand carried a huge responsibility.

It was this type of circumstance that made me miss my mother the most. Prior to her passing, she was the one I could bare my soul to and get honest feedback from. She was my confidant. We would always discuss the topic at hand and come to a mutual understanding. As her life became shorter and shorter, the subject of the hereafter became a more constant conversation. We both believed she could contact me after her death, and we agreed on a sign. Whenever a light flickered, I knew she was watching over me and that I should read my daily devotional for higher guidance.

What on earth made me ever consider answering a classified ad that began "Seeker of fortune's angel" without first reaching out for confirmed acceptance from those watching out for me from above? When I arrived home, I had my answer as I read the following: "Trust and be not afraid. Life is full of wonder. Open childlike, trusting eyes to all I am doing for you. Fear not. You are now walking in the tunnel darkness. Soon you shall see light to guide feet that are afraid."

CHAPTER 2

M ICHAEL WAS THE PERFECT neighbor to have in my apartment complex. He showed a caring exuberance for life, yet he never asked too many questions. He could be trusted with my cell phone number and to stop by my place to feed Missy, the kitty, when I opted to stay over at Mandie's place. The latter seemed to happen more often as of late, and I almost felt the need for more conversation when meeting him in the parking lot.

"Hey, Carrie, what's going on?" he shouted from three cars over.

As we approached each other, Shiloh's body motion in my arms and gentle whimpering confirmed what a nice guy Michael truly was. The three of us did our normal group hug, and we started laughing as we broke away from a short reenactment of long-lost friends.

"Not much on this end," I said with a shrug, "Just came back from the library to check out a book and any possible leads online." The one thing I prided myself in being was frugal, and there certainly was no sense in paying for classifieds or an Internet hookup if the library was only a few blocks away. "Cross your fingers for me," I said, "I've got a lead on a job, and I'm hoping for an interview. That reminds me: if I land this job, I'll be doing some traveling fairly soon, so any chance you can make sure Missy doesn't find my absence too bothersome?"

"No prob, neighbor!" he said with a smile.

What a nice guy. Almost too nice. If I could ever share my innermost secrets and open my heart up again to someone, this would be the man. Michael was the kind of guy who caught your eye immediately. His tall, tan frame and athletic torso actually seemed to make one's mind drift off to a Bahamas vacation commercial. One couldn't help but notice his white teeth and smile. Irresistible smile. Of course, it helped that his blond hair—almost white from the sun—was longer than the hair of most men in their thirties. He was easy to talk to, unattached, and worked out of his apartment ... so those factors made him a perfect neighbor.

"Key in the same place?" he quizzed.

I nodded as we headed up the stairwell to our adjoining front doors. "Thanks again for being so supportive," I said, meaning every word, "I'll give you a call if and when I leave."

As we both entered our respective apartments, I could finally close the door behind me and settle into the enormous task at hand. Setting Shiloh and my bookbag down, I was able to pull out my library rental. The large letters jumped out at me: *ROME. Please, dear God, let this be the first step in landing this new job!* My prayer was interrupted by my phone ringing. I smiled when I saw it was my good friend Mandie.

CHAPTER 3

I<small>T HAD ALWAYS AMAZED</small> me how in tune Mandie and I were with each other. Our lives, at least for the past thirteen years, had always been parallel. The heavens above must have known it was destiny for us to meet and placed us on the same page of life's occurrences. Whatever happened to one of us happened almost immediately to the other, thereby giving us the walk-in-my-shoes understanding on any given day.

Caring by nature, Mandie's natural balance was upset only by happenchance. She was always the one person I could talk to, the one who would help me rationalize, analyze, and come to a better understanding of self. I could not hope for a more loyal friend. That stated, she was also the one I turned to for a traveling companion, seeker of fine wines, love adviser, and dogsitter.

Her blonde hair and recently formed Pilates body made her the absolute perfect friend. All eyes tended to follow her, thereby allowing me to simply disappear in any given setting. We could not be more different in our outward appearances. My dark hair and tall, thin frame—along with my constant wardrobe of boy shorts and simple tees—seemed to let men think I wouldn't be too much of a challenge in today's competitive world. She was strikingly beautiful and graceful, which left me always looking for a tennis partner.

If I were in the business of matchmaking, I would have suggested Michael to her. Even though we tended to share most everything with each other, I still had not made the introduction yet. Time would tell if and when I decided to share my hidden treasure.

"Hey, girlfriend," she said, "What's happening in your world?"

"I am so glad you called, Mandie-girl. You and I have to talk, but I don't want to do it over the phone. Any shot at heading my way today? I have something to tell you, and you aren't going to believe it. The heavens just opened up for me, and I need your logical thoughts on it."

"Now you really have me intrigued," Mandie said, "Is one hour soon enough?"

"Perfect," I said anxiously, "One hour until I can tell you about the most interesting ad I found in the paper—and how I am hoping you can help me decipher it."

CHAPTER 4

A<small>S WE SIPPED ON</small> some Riesling, I filled Mandie in on the past few days. "I have been checking the classifieds, as you know, and yesterday I came upon a new one I almost missed. I had to read it a couple of times before I actually understood the content. At least I think I understand the content. Anyway, you know how most employers simply list the position and what type of individual would be ideal? This particular one simply said, 'Seeker of fortune's angel. Must be charismatic, unattached, trustworthy, relentless, willing to travel. Salary commensurate with cleverness. Inquire at library. *Buona fortuna.'*"

Mandie's look was one of disbelief. "You must be kidding! You aren't telling me you answered this ad?"

"Yes, oh yes, dear friend. This is the very ad I answered," I said with affirmation.

Her comeback was instantaneous: "But how?"

"Well," I said, "contrary to public opinion, I do have some cleverness hidden away. Close your mouth or take another sip of wine ... and settle in." As we both flopped onto my beanbag chairs, I could see the wonder in her eyes.

"If you don't start talking, I'm going to strangle you," Mandie said with a raised voice.

She was right; I had let it go way too long without sharing the facts.

"I headed over to the library this morning knowing that it was one of the two clues given in the ad," I said as I lowered my voice, "Once I got there, I headed to the travel section."

"Give me a break," Mandie said, "You knew to head to the travel section?"

"But of course, my dear Watson," I said with a smirk, "The ad specifically said I needed to be willing to travel."

"Go on. This better be good," she said with doubt in her voice.

I continued my adventure: "As I walked up and down the aisles, it jumped out at me. I should head to the section marked *Italy*."

"Why?" Mandie questioned with a laugh.

"Because the other clue in the ad was *buona fortuna*," I said, emphasizing the last two words. The light went on in her eyes, and she stood up and said, "Italian for good luck."

"Right you are," I said as I gave her a high five.

Mandie's questions were not yet finished. She said, "But how did you know which book to pick out?"

"This is where my cleverness comes in," I said with a smug look. "I thought and thought before it occurred to me. I went over the ad again, word by word. 'Seeker of fortune's angel.' *Angel.* Where are the most angels in Italy? Rome. This book had the biggest *Rome* title on it." I wasn't sure what to expect from Mandie, but my wildest expectations were met when her eyes got huge and her mouth dropped open.

"You went to the library's travel section, picked out the country of Italy, came home with a book from Rome, and assumed you would somehow get a job offer for doing all of this?"

"Are you going to let me finish?" I said with my Cheshire cat smile. "I then sat down and opened up the book. While thumbing through the pages, I found picture after picture of basilicas, museums, the Vatican, and one full-page picture of an angel. I felt certain this was my best clue, and I brought the book home so you and I could figure out the missing piece of the puzzle. I just know we can find a way to contact the person who wrote this ad."

Mandie already had the book in hand, and she was checking out each picture, page by page. Her ability to logically think through a situation was second to none, and it really didn't surprise me when I saw her reaching for pen and paper.

"Maybe there's a connection between the page number, copyright date, and which edition it is. If I look for numbers that coincide with our local prefix, perhaps we can come up with the last four numbers to start randomly dialing," said Mandie, pulling out a chair.

Within minutes she was handing me her page with seven numbers on it.

CHAPTER 5

I T DIDN'T TAKE VERY long to wade through the different combinations. I was actually feeding Missy with the phone resting on my shoulder when, after about the tenth try, an elderly male voice answered. Because I had either gotten disconnected recordings or message units on all the previous tries, his voice caught me off guard.

"Ah, hello," I said, astonished I even heard a voice on the other end of the phone line. "This may sound like a foolish question, but you didn't happen to place an ad in the paper recently, did you?"

Mandie was also caught off guard, and she came running back into the room the minute she heard my question. It was like time stood still before an answer came over the phone waves.

"Who is calling, please?" he asked with shortness of breath.

"This is Carrie Lamm, sir, and I'm so sorry to bother you."

"You aren't bothering me, young lady. One might actually say that I have been waiting for your call."

As surreal as it sounded, it immediately brought me back to earth, and I felt my heart start to race. "You've been waiting for me to call, sir?"

About this time, Mandie was dancing up and down, and her eyes were questioning my every reply.

"Yes," he said, clearing his voice. "Would it be asking too much for you to visit with me in person?"

His question to me was interrupted with intervals of coughing and wheezing, which led me to ask again whether he was all right and whether there was anything I might do to help him.

"My dear, the one thing you could do to help me would be to accept my invitation to dinner this evening."

My immediate answer surprised even myself. Did I actually accept an invitation from someone I had only talked over the phone with for three minutes? Perhaps it was my mother who had developed my strong faith in mankind. She always thought the best of everyone, and I could hear her voice saying, "Faith is the daring of the soul to go further than it can see." It was her urging I felt, and it was her insistence that, if the door was open, you should walk through it.

Mandie, on the other hand, thought I had lost it. "Did I really just hear you accept an invitation from a complete stranger? I don't care how important this specific job is to you, you are not going outside this apartment unless I go with you."

"Oh my gosh, Mandie, it's just dinner. And the man sounds old enough to be my grandfather. You, above anyone, should realize how I've tapped into my savings and how desperately I need a job. And not just any job. I need a job with a purpose, or I just can't go to work day after day. Besides, you'll have to admit, we just had the best time being super sleuths, and think about it: the combination of my cleverness and your ingenuity landed me this puzzling interview."

Mandie's next question caught me off guard: "And your point?"

I finally understood her concern, and I said, "C'mon, you know I'm not always a risk taker, but if you insist, I'll call him back and ask if my friend can accompany me."

"Perfect. Call him back, and I'll head home to change," Mandie said, acting as though she had won the lottery. "What time should I be back?"

"Make it 7:00 so it gives us some time to find his house," I said and headed for the shower.

CHAPTER 6

B OTH OF US WERE pleasantly surprised to find ourselves driving around one of the oldest, yet most prestigous, neighborhoods south of town. Lawndale was definitely equal to none. The homes were huge, the yards were well-manicured, and the streets seemed to meander into cul-de-sacs and turnarounds. It actually made you feel like you had gone back in time—perhaps years ago, when neighbors actually knew one another. Front doors were open, allowing the spring winds to purify cooking odors. No curbs were formed, lending bicycles easy access to both sidewalks and streets. Fences were nonexistent, and Mandie and I kept noticing dogs lounging on front stoops and cats walking leisurely over vibrant green lawns. Each home was unique, and within minutes, we found ourselves in front of an exceptional-looking French country manor. A weeping willow graced the front yard, and I could not help but notice the large cement angel at the base of the tree.

"This is it," I said as I turned off my 1991 Olds Cutlass. I truly found comfort in the car. It had been driven just over one hundred thousand miles, and my mother was the original owner. It was her wish to give it to me after she passed, and each and every time I pulled the sun visor down, I saw one of the last pictures I took of her at the care center. Mom had kept this beauty spotless, and I found myself replacing new parts when they went out rather than adding an additional car payment to my monthly bills. I thought, *Perhaps, if I land this job, I can actually think about purchasing a new hybrid.*

As we opened our car doors and started walking up the long, flower-lined sidewalk, Mandie quizzed me once again: "Are you sure you want to go through with this?"

"Of course I want to go through with this," I said, "Who wouldn't want to check out the inside of this gorgeous country home and meet my possible new employer?"

We approached the front door, and I turned back to watch a police car driving slowly. The police officer was turning his head back and forth from home to home. *How great to be wealthy enough to have your own neighborhood patrol during the day,* I thought.

I rang the doorbell and was pleasantly reminded of the church bells at Immaculate Conception Church before each mass. *It's strange how music and perfume or cologne always takes me back in time. I was told many years ago that most of us remember where we were or what we were doing when a certain scent or sound touches our senses, and I definitely believe that statement.* As the door opened, a thin-built, older gentlemen with somber facial features appeared.

"May I help you?" he asked. There was absolutely no doubt (based on his uniform) that he was some kind of servant or butler or whichever kind of person rich people hire to answer their doors.

"Yes, my name is Carrie, and this is Mandie. We were invited to dinner this evening."

The room we were taken to was as big as my entire apartment. The walls were lined with bookshelves, and to my surprise, I spotted a ladder halfway down one wall. I knew from the movies that it must have been used to climb up to reach a certain book.

Mandie took the words right out of my mouth: "Now this is what a home library should look like. Do you think we can get a tour of the rest of the house?"

"Focus, girlfriend, focus," I said while walking back and forth and reading book titles, "You aren't going to believe this, but all of these books are arranged in sections, and each section is arranged alphabetically. Wow, just look at this collection of written matter."

I was just starting to pull a book from a shelf when I heard the door behind us open. I found myself staring at a very elderly gentleman in a wheelchair. He seemed to have no problem letting his hands turn the wheels to enter the room, but I noticed an oxygen breathing device hooked onto both ears and extending into his nostrils. As pale as his skin looked—and as tiny as his frame was—he still made me feel like he had been a towering figure in his day. His eyes were deep blue, and they never left my eyes from the moment he entered the room. They say that first impressions are important, and there was no doubt in my mind that the person before me was a caring soul. He just seemed to radiate a soothing presence, which made me smile as I said, "Hi, I'm Carrie. This is my friend, Mandie, sir."

"Nice to meet both of you. Please call me Dr. Gabel and have a seat." His eyebrows arched upward as he looked directly at me and said, "So you are the very clever gal who figured out my newspaper listing?"

I nodded and added, "Along with my friend's help to retrieve your phone number."

"I'll get right to the point," he said in a soft voice, "I am in need of someone who is talkative yet discreet, sensitive yet spirited, ambitious yet not willing to compromise. Do any of these attributes sound like you?"

"Actually, sir, they do," I said confidently. I felt my face start to flush.

"Do you believe in a higher power and destiny, Carrie?"

"I do, sir."

I'm not sure why, but his next words put me at ease: "By wording my ad the way I did, I was hopeful someone with faith would be, at the very least, intrigued by my use of the word *angel*. Do you think it is a coincidence that you are the only one answering my oddly worded want ad? I think not. What made you answer it?"

I answered from my heart and said, "The cryptic wording and use of the word *angel* seemed to speak directly to me. I must admit, though, I also was intrigued by the fact that I could compete with the multitudes to win a chance at a job interview and the possibility of traveling."

"I can find anyone to travel," he said, coughing into his hand, "I need to find someone who believes in what they are doing and who is willing to proceed on my guidance. That special someone needs to be willing to go out on a limb for a just cause. One would need to follow through with their convictions until the business dealing is complete. Does this continue to sound like something you would like to pursue?"

CHAPTER 7

I WAS THANKFUL HE allowed me to think about his question over dinner and ponder the many questions I had regarding the position he was attempting to fill. The dining room decor continued the theme of French country living. The large, rectangular dining table had a low-sheen finish, and it sat directly under a wrought iron chandelier. Carved details graced the ladder-back dining chairs, and the flooring of wooden boards definitely gave it an old world look. Still, it was very charming. Lush natural flowers were everywhere in baskets, copper pots, and old pitchers. Colorful pottery adorned the table setting, and one could immediately tell that a woman had once graced the beautiful home.

We were seated across from Dr. Gabel, and I could not help but notice the artwork on the walls.

"I see you value the French impressionist, Claude Monet, Doctor," I said, proud that I knew great art.

Dr. Gabel openly smiled as he said, "I have been fortunate to travel quite extensively in my lifetime, and I have been able to acquire lovely paintings. It pleases me that you are aware of your surroundings. Are you at liberty to travel at will, Ms. Carrie?"

"Yes, sir," I answered, "Am I to assume I would be traveling to Italy for you?"

I could tell Dr. Gabel was tiring fast, but he answered my question: "That is correct. Italy is the first country. You see, I have something I would like to give to an individual in Rome. It's my desire that someone interacts with this person over a short period of time, thereby authenticating the need for my gift."

My mind was racing. "It would seem there is more involved than me just being your liaison. Am I to assume this person will be unaware who I am?"

Dr. Gabel raised his eyebrows, came forward in his chair, placed his elbows on the table, and with a very optimistic tone in his voice said, "Yes, this is where some skill comes into play. Let me just say that deception will be needed to complete this business dealing. I have no intention of doing anything illegal or immoral—nor will I ask that of you. You will be at liberty to use your innovative persona in order to achieve our mutual goal. A kind heart, intuition, and faith will play a large part in this position."

I was hoping I wasn't getting too personal when I asked, "Why the reference to an angel in your ad?"

Dr. Gabel's eyes looked upward and off to the right as he said, "I was orphaned at an early age. I would pray daily to my guardian angel to bring a loving mother and father into my world. When I was four years old, I was placed into a very adoring home. I feel angels have surrounded me ever since, and I pray on a daily basis to them. Since angels cannot fly down from on high, I have decided to extend my faith out to the public and hire my own earthly angel to help me fulfill my dreams before I leave this earth."

"Is there more you can share?" I asked sheepishly, "You definitely have my attention, Doctor."

"If you were to be under my employ, you would have all your expenses paid while actually on the job. I would give you a portfolio to read to prepare you ahead of time for your assignment. You would then have the liberty to become whoever you wish to become to facilitate the goal at hand. Of course, I would expect complete confidentiality, and you would (at no time) be able to divulge my rationale behind this gift. My name would always remain in strict confidence. We would communicate as needed until the end of our joint journey. Do you have further questions?"

My eyes were wide like a schoolgirl's when I said, "Just one. When can I start?"

CHAPTER 8

MANDIE STARTED TALKING THE very moment we walked out the front door. She said, "Tell me how you do it."

"Tell you what?" I asked, knowing exactly what she meant.

"How you find a perfect want ad, undergo a perfect interview with a perfect boss, and make a life decision in one perfect hour?" By the time she finished her sentence, Mandie was smiling ear to ear and giving me high fives before we reached the car.

"Pinch me," I said, "I actually feel as though this is a dream." *Thank you, God, for giving me the chance to be Dr. Gabel's angel-in-waiting.*

Mandie's voice got low as she said, "Ah, excuse me. Don't you think you are getting a tad bit ahead of the game? You can thank God after we receive the portfolio, and that happens only after he checks you out to make sure you aren't a crazy want ad person."

Mandie's laugh was infectious, and the two of us didn't stop until the car pulled into my apartment complex.

"Let me know when you know anything. Sleep well, and I'll pray this all works out for you," Mandie said.

CHAPTER 9

I HADN'T BEEN HOME more than thirty minutes when I heard a knock at my door. Of course, Shiloh made it a point to let me know someone was intruding into our private world. It was 10:30. I wasn't really excited about answering the door because I had already slipped out of my clothes and into a short tee and gym shorts. After a quick glance through my peephole, a look of surprise came over my face.

As I was opening the door, I heard Michael saying, "Before you get after me for it being so late, know I bring food and drink."

"Who could resist a man bearing gifts?" I asked with a smirk, "Step right into my lair."

As I looked at Michael, the thought occurred to me that I looked pretty basic, and he looked like he just stepped out of a Mr. Clean commercial. I said, without hesitating, "You look great, and I look, well, not so great. You'll have to excuse me, but I was just about ready to head off to never-never land."

Michael's eyes gleamed as he said, "You look pretty darn great to me. Matter of fact, you can wear that outfit any day of the week—and certainly anytime I drop by."

By this time, I was blushing. I just motioned him into the living room and plopped down on the couch. Before I could settle in, my right hand felt a wine opener from when Mandie had been over, and I tossed it up. He snatched it midair.

"Good catch," I said, meaning it.

"Good throw," he said as he started opening the wine he brought over. "Hope you don't mind me eating cold pizza in front of you."

For a second, my mind wandered off to my dinner with Dr. Gabel. I really wanted to share what had transpired just hours earlier. My thoughts were interrupted when Michael said, "Aren't you supposed to ask me why I'm here?"

"Okay, why are you here?" I asked as I covered my mouth to hide a yawn.

"You told me you had a lead for a job and a possible interview, and I couldn't sleep without hearing how it went," he said with a boyish grin.

"Actually, my entire evening went quite well," I said as I picked up my first piece of pizza. "I was just thinking I might get your feedback on this probable job offer."

I noticed Michael's entire body relax as he heard I might share some of my world with him. He actually relaxed so much that he missed the wine glass completely while pouring the merlot. Red wine managed to find its way to my carpeting. I found myself shouting, "Watch out!" right as he noticed his mistake. Both of us ran to the kitchen for a towel, and we bumped into one another in the process. I landed on my back and looked up to find Michael's tan frame right on top of me. He was able to catch most of his weight on his arms, and within seconds, I found myself inches from his face. I knew his eyes were blue, but not Brad Pitt blue. I knew his cheek bones were pronounced, but not *so* prominent. I had been close to him before, but not that close.

I had never actually thought about kissing Michael, but then again, he had never fallen on top of me before. His lips felt smooth. My heart was racing, and I had no intention of being the first one to break away. My eyes were closed and I never wanted to open them again. The moment was perfect. Seconds passed, and I felt as though I were in a dream. Shiloh, however, brought me back to reality as he started barking while running back and forth around the two of us. The little guy must have thought I was hurt. It didn't take Michael long to realize what was happening, and he immediately pulled away from me.

Michael's voice was soothing as he said, "Shiloh, it's all right, little guy. Nothing is wrong. I was just talking *very close* to your mom."

Funny how I had never noticed the dimple in his left cheek before that moment. *It must be more pronounced when he is holding back a laugh,* I thought. In any case, for a few seconds, I felt that awkward moment—the kind I felt when the paperboy noticed me watching him when I was thirteen. I was still thinking about that unexpected kiss when he reached down to help me up.

"Thanks," I said. "We'd better hurry up and find a towel or we'll both be paying for a carpet cleaner."

Within seconds, he grabbed a towel and tossed it back to me to start blotting my tan carpeting. I heard Michael playing with Shiloh behind me by throwing his chew toy back and forth across the floor. Hearing his laugh made me feel quite content, but I certainly wasn't about to fall head over heals again. He was the perfect neighbor, and I wasn't about to ruin our friendship over one kiss … even if it was fantastic.

Michael headed back to his place after about thirty minutes, and I could not wait to head to my bedroom for further thought. Upon entering, I noticed my night-light, which illuminated my porcelain angel, going off and on. A smile came over my face as I reached for my devotional and read, "Your path is difficult. There is no work in life so hard as waiting, and yet I say to wait. Wait until I show you My will."

CHAPTER 10

My mind wandered over the next few days. Surely, Dr. Gabel would have my background checked and find I was the perfect one to help him with his upcoming project. After all, I had never even gotten so much as a speeding ticket in my young life. I had prided myself in always being in the top ten in all my classes, and I had excelled in the business world. I had even considered enlisting in the peace corps right out of college, but I changed my mind when my mother was diagnosed with Alzheimer's. Perhaps, he thought I seemed too needy or too young. I always hated this part of life—the not knowing part. I didn't like the insecure person I became when I had no control over what life had to offer.

"Settle in, little guy," I said to Shiloh who was turning around and around on my lap, "Let me finish writing out these bills, and we'll go for a walk."

I had barely finished my sentence when he jumped off my lap and ran over to the door. I have always marveled at the acute hearing of animals. Shiloh's head was turning back and forth to adjust to whatever or whomever he heard in the parking lot.

"What do you hear, little guy?" I said, slightly inconvenienced by the interruption.

My curiosity was satisfied when I heard the doorbell ring. As I walked over to pick up Shiloh, I checked the peephole. The UPS gal who handled our neighborhood was on the other side.

"I have a package that needs your signature, Carrie," she said, with a smile.

"Great, let me sign that for you. I suppose this is your favorite time of year to be outside on your deliveries, right?"

"Right," she said, as she handed me a pretty large box. "Enjoy your day."

The box was heavier than I expected, and I actually needed to put Shiloh down to carry it inside. I wasn't sure what to think, so I looked to see who had sent it. I immediately recognized the part of town: Lawndale.

Please, Lord, let this be what I hope it is. I flew inside and placed the box on my dining room table. It didn't take long before I was tearing at the brown paper to find a white box about the size of a photo album. All four sides were carefully taped, and I slit each piece with my thumbnail before pulling the top off. My eyes rested on a handwritten note: "Carrie: The Divine Voice is not always expressed in words. It is made known as a heart-consciousness. My heart is telling me you are perfect to be my liaison. Please read this portfolio, and I will be contacting you shortly. Dr. Gabel"

CHAPTER 11

I GRABBED A DIET coke, fluffed my pillows, and nestled down on the top of my bed. Shiloh immediately jumped up and found his way between the comforter and my feet. The front of the three-ring binder was devoid of writing, and I had it open in a matter of seconds. The inside was divided into sections labeled *Specifics, Background, Rationale,* and *Unknown Factors.*

I never stopped reading until I turned the last page of the portfolio, and I'm certain several hours passed. It was as if it were a murder mystery, and I couldn't put it down before the case was solved. *Good grief, I hope I haven't agreed to a task more challenging than I can pull off,* I thought. That insecurity was sneaking out again. The sun was going down in the bedroom, and my stomach told me I needed the lasagna from the fridge. Hopefully a break from reading would give me a new perspective.

I decided to take the plastic container of pasta along with me as Shiloh and I went on our normal trek around the block. I had gotten pretty good at eating with one hand and holding the leash with the other. The trick was answering my phone if it rang—it always seemed to define my dexterity. About halfway around the block, my cell went off, and I heard Taylor Swift's "Our Song." *I smile every time I hear it. I'm such a romantic.*

"Hello," I said, not knowing who was calling (I couldn't see the screen with the phone upside down).

"Hello, yourself," was Michael's answer, "I didn't get you eating, did I?"

"Actually, you got me walking Shiloh and eating," I said laughing, "What's going on?"

"My brother just left me a present on his way through town," Michael said, "I was thinking it might be something you could use since I already have one."

"Now that'll get my interest," I said, "What is it?"

Michael's answer was like a gift from heaven: "His laptop computer. He doesn't need it anymore since he just bought a new notebook."

"Give me ten minutes, and I'll be knocking down your door," I said laughing.

"Great. I'll leave the door unlocked."

Chapter 12

IN NO TIME, I was back home and tossing some food in Shiloh's dish. I checked in the mirror to find my hair somewhat matted. I pulled a brush through it and applied some fresh lipstick. I tossed on one of my newer T-shirts and grabbed Dr. Gabel's portfolio. It was going on fifteen minutes when I reached Michael's door.

"Knock, knock," I said as I entered his apartment.

Michael came out of the kitchen with a bottle of wine in his hand and said, "Hey, you." He shot me a big smile—that irresistible smile.

"Where's this computer you are willing to share with me?" I asked.

"Over on the desk," he said, "It's only a couple years old, and if you give me the go ahead, I'll set it up for you."

As I headed over to his desk, he noticed the three-ring binder under my arm.

"I brought this over to get your feedback on my latest job prospect," I said. "After we check out your brother's computer, perhaps we can sit down and go over some of my thoughts."

"Super," he said. He then proceeded to tell me all about the computer, and my mind started imagining how great it would be for my upcoming trip to Italy. I asked him, "Would you be able to receive e-mails from me even if I leave the country?"

"Of course, Carrie. I would love to receive e-mails from you wherever you travel," Michael said with a sincere look on his face.

"Good, because you could be my sounding board when I'm on my first assignment in Italy," I replied.

Michael could not have looked more sincere when he said, "Have a seat. Let's go over what you have in that book of yours. We don't have to wait until you head out of the country for me to be your sounding board. Let me put some popcorn in the microwave so that we can almost consider it a date."

CHAPTER 13

B Y THE TIME WE had gone over the portfolio from front to back, it was
well past midnight. As I turned the last page, both of us looked at each
other in amazement. It was Michael who broke the silence first by saying,
"Good God, I feel like I'm in the middle of an espionage plot! What kind
of individual knows *this much* about someone in another country? And
the better question, my dear: what are you supposed to do with all this
information?"

"I'm supposed to verify this individual is who he says he is."

"Okay," Michael said, "but how do you intend to do that?"

"By entering into his world without him knowing I'm checking him out,"
I said with a smug look on my face. "This is the neat part of my job. I get to
impersonate whoever I want in order to gain his confidence and make sure
he is the real deal."

Michael looked skeptical and said, "You are sure this is on the up and
up, right?"

"Actually, I hadn't thought about checking out Dr. Gabel until you just
now mentioned it," I said sheepishly.

"Well, then, that's why we have a computer in front of us. Let's do that
very thing right now," Michael said.

CHAPTER 14

As MICHAEL WENT TO work letting his fingers do the walking, I settled in on his couch and grabbed one of his throws. It had been a long day—especially long since the arrival of Dr. Gabel's box. I just needed to close my eyes for a minute and try to put everything into perspective. I was still a little in awe that I was the chosen one, and I needed to attempt to put everything in some kind of order. Speaking of order, I definitely needed to call Mandie in the morning and get her read on everything. She was truly the one who could rationalize.

"Carrie, wake up. Are you going to sleep your life away?" Michael's voice sounded as though it were in my dream, and I continued laying there until I felt a nudge on my elbow.

"Okay, already. I'm awake," I said as I sat up and held back a yawn. The sun coming in his living room window told me immediately that I had spent the night on Michael's couch. "What time is it?"

"Eight o'clock, Saturday morning," he said with a smile.

"Oh my gosh, I must have fallen asleep. What do I smell?" I asked him.

"You smell my mother's egg casserole recipe."

"Boy, oh boy, does that sound super good," I said jumping up from the couch, "How about me heading to my place to grab Shiloh for a walk, take a quick shower, and return to eat whatever is sending that delicious aroma throughout your apartment?"

Michael's look told me I needed to slow down and listen. I used to see that same look on my dad's face during my teenage years.

"Okay," I said, "what am I missing?"

Michael said his next sentence very slow and methodically: "I was up until 3 a.m. on the Internet searching every source known to man to find out about your Dr. Gabel. As far as I can tell—and I'm certain when I say this—your Dr. Gabel does not exist ... at least not on paper."

You could have thrown a rock at me and I wouldn't have moved. I finally said, "You are telling me that I have just accepted a paying position from a gentlemen who has no paper trail at all?"

"That's exactly what I'm telling you," Michael said.

CHAPTER 15

I HADN'T BEEN OUT the door with Shiloh more than thirty seconds before I was dialing Mandie on her cell. "Get your butt over here because I really, really need your thoughts, Mandie-girl," I said when I got her voice mail. "Come over when you hear this message."

Ordinarily, I walked Shiloh at a fairly fast pace, but my mind was so active that I just wanted to take my time so I could attempt to visualize my next move. *How can Dr. Gabel not exist? He certainly looked real. His home certainly seemed real. Lord, please tell me I'm not dreaming all of this!*

Before I could think worse thoughts, my cell rang. It was Mandie.

"Hey, I'm heading your way now. Everything all right?" she questioned.

"Not really, but it'll wait until you get here. If I don't answer my door, knock on the apartment across from mine, okay?" I said quickly.

"You got it," Mandie said and hung up.

I showered in record time, and I headed back over to Michael's place. I found him in the kitchen, taking out the egg casserole.

"I told you I'd return to the scene of the crime," I said as I walked toward him.

"Find yourself a chair and sit down. Before we discuss my findings—or lack thereof—we both need some sustenance," Michael said.

The food was just what I needed to get my old self back into gear. The more I ate, the more I calmed down. I could literally feel my muscles relaxing.

"Okay," I said after I had polished off an entire plate of egg casserole, "That was to die for, and I am eternally grateful. Moving right along, perhaps Dr. Gabel recently moved into the state. Perhaps your search engine didn't find him because he's new to the area."

"Nope. I did a full search. I even dropped thirty bucks to see whether he had a police record," Michael said with a stern face. "If this man is who he says he is, he's covered his tracks pretty darn good."

"Lovely," I said with a frown, "Mandie, my girlfriend, is on her way over here, and I'm going to suggest we call him back and confront him. Do you think that's a good idea?"

"I sure don't like the word *confront*," Michael said, "Perhaps I've just missed something on my computer."

"Or perhaps he isn't the man he represented himself to be," I said emphatically. "I was so looking forward to Italy. But wait a minute, why would he give me all this personal information on another individual if he wasn't who he says he is? I don't know what to think now."

CHAPTER 16

HEARING A KNOCK ON Michael's door told me Mandie had arrived. As he headed to let her in, I started gathering our breakfast plates and attempted to do a fast wash in the sink. The two of them were already seated in the living room when I walked up.

"Hey, guess I don't have to do the introductions, right?" I asked chuckling.

"No," Mandie said, "we've already done them. So what's going on?"

As I started relaying the events of the past twelve hours, Michael mentioned he was heading into the shower. That gave Mandie and me more than enough time to discuss not only the notebook I received, but also Dr. Gabel's lack of Internet information.

Mandie was paging through the portfolio and said, "It just doesn't make any sense. Dr. Gable wouldn't give you all this information on someone if he wasn't on the up and up. What if Michael never suggested you check out your source? What if you two never thought to search for information about him? There has to be a good reason why this doctor isn't a high-profile guy. I think you are freaking out for no reason."

"I just knew you would calm my senses. So you think Dr. Gabel is okay?" I asked.

"He seemed perfectly fine to me the night we met him. Of course, we don't even know if he's a medical doctor or professor, do we?" Mandie questioned, "Maybe we should drive over to his house on the premise that you need to ask about something in the portfolio he sent you. That way, we could direct the conversation to his past and present life."

"The information he sent me on this Angelo Giovanni is pretty detailed. I guess I could think of some question for Dr. Gabel, but I'm the one who supposedly is *clever*, remember?" I said standing up.

Our thoughts were interrupted when Michael walked into the room. Whatever cologne he was wearing agreed totally with my sense of smell. He had shorts with a pressed T-shirt on, and he looked like a million fresh dollars. Of course, he led with his smile, and I couldn't resist checking out Mandie's expression to see whether he caught her eye too. A foolish thought—of course he caught both of her eyes.

"So, ladies, what's the plan for Carrie's doctor friend?" Michael asked.

"We were thinking we might head back to his house to question him on some trivial matter just to be able to explore more of the world of the little known Dr. Gabel," Mandie said with a complacent look.

"What are we waiting for, then?" Michael said with authority.

The three of us looked at each other, stood up, and started for the door.

"Let me grab the portfolio so I can come up with a question on our drive to Lawndale," I said.

CHAPTER 17

B Y THE TIME WE pulled up to his house, I had figured out a question, and I was more than eager to lay all of our doubts to rest. I was attempting to put the pages back into numerical order when the thought hit me: *Why haven't Mandie and Michael opened their car doors?*

Michael broke the silence by asking, "You are sure this is the right house?"

I looked up to check it out, and both Mandie and I said in unison: "Of course we're sure this is the right house. Why are you doubting it?"

"Because," he said, "this house looks empty. Curtains closed over most of the windows, a newspaper thrown on the lawn, and the porch light left on."

That sinking feeling hit both Mandie and me at the same time, and I could read her thoughts as she looked directly into my eyes from the front seat.

"I know this is the house," I said, "There's the weeping willow tree and the cement angel."

"Get out of the car, y'all, and let's walk up to the house," Mandie said.

The three of us jumped out of the car, and we were on the front lawn in a nanosecond. Mandie and I headed toward the door while Michael stooped down to pick up the newspaper.

"Yesterday's date on the paper," he said.

"Just knock on the door and quit acting like this is a scene from the *Twilight Zone*," Mandie whispered.

I reached for the brass knocker and pounded twice. Nothing. The three of us stood there looking at each other, and I knocked even louder. Nothing. As if out of a Hitchcock movie, we all walked to separate windows and looked in through the glass.

"The library looks the same to me," I said with certainty.

"The dining room looks the same to me," Mandie said.

"The living room has sheets covering all the furniture," Michael said, sounding like a TV detective.

That one statement sent chills up my arms. Sheets on the furniture? Why would anyone cover their furniture unless they had left the premises? Why would they leave so soon, and why would Dr. Gabel not have told me he was leaving? There were too many questions left unanswered, and too many theories left rambling around in my head.

I finally broke the silence by saying, "I'm going to call him on my cell and tell him we're outside his house." My fingers had his number dialed in seconds, and the look on my face must have been mind-boggling as I heard the recorded message telling me the number had been disconnected.

"I don't even have to ask," Mandie said, "The number isn't a working one, is it?"

CHAPTER 18

I COULD NOT HELP but read my devotional as soon as I walked into my apartment. If I ever had needed reassurance from above, this was the time. I read the words aloud: "Do not forget to meet all your difficulties with love and laughter. Be assured that I am with you. Remember, it is the last few yards that tell. Not one of your cries is unheard."

I knew I had been quiet on the ride home—even more quiet after I told Mandie and Michael to head back to their places so I could think about the last several hours before doing anything. I almost felt betrayed. The feeling would not leave me until I started to meditate on the words found in my prayer book. It told me outright to be patient. My faith kicked into gear, and from that moment on, I found peace. I concentrated on Dr. Gabel's portfolio and thought through the process of entering into Angelo Giovanni's life.

The knock on my door interrupted my concentration (as well as Shiloh's nap). With a quick check to see who was on the other side, I opened the door to find the same UPS gal who had delivered the portfolio a few days earlier. As I signed for the large envelope, I once again noticed the return address was Dr. Gabel's. It didn't take me long before I had it open and began staring at airline tickets, a driver's license, a passport, and travelers checks. The one thing they all had in common was the name on each. The curious part was that it wasn't my name.

It didn't take me long to find his letter. It was concise: "Please find enclosed your new identity. I will contact you next in Rome. *Buona Fortuna.*"

CHAPTER 19

THE NEXT FEW DAYS felt like a whirlwind. I thanked Michael a dozen times for getting my new laptop working. I was able to use it to check temperatures in Italy, how much luggage I could take, and specifics for traveling with a dog. By the time I had finished all my running around, a couple days had passed. I was more than anxious to get on my way. Both Shiloh and Missy knew something was up with suitcases everywhere, and they refused to let me out of their sight.

"You have cash for tipping, right?" Mandie asked as she placed all my toiletries into clear bags.

"Check," I said with a smile.

"Your laptop that you promise to use to e-mail often, right?" Mandie asked.

"Double check," I said.

"Are you sure you don't want me to find you a hotel and make a reservation?" Mandie asked for the second time.

"I think I'll be fine," I answered, "The list you gave me of hotels that accept dogs will do for now. I'd kind of like to check out where our heir apparent lives and works and get a place close by."

As Mandie went around my apartment checking everything I was taking to Italy, she noticed my tennis racket leaning next to the front door. "Are you taking this?" she asked, surprised to see it.

"Check," I said, with a gleam in my eyes. "That is the one item that is getting me both a job and a way to meet our heir apparent."

"That's right. Kind of neat to play Superman and change into whoever you want to be for the good of ... what's it for the good of?" Mandie asked with a puzzled look on her face.

"To help humankind," I said with resolve.

It took less than an hour before the suitcases were closed, the blinds were open for my plants, Shiloh was in his carrier, and Missy had additional toys scattered around. I picked up my cell and left a message for Michael saying he was officially on cat duty.

I knew Mandie and Michael didn't have the enthusiasm I had for this new liaison position, but I assured both of them I was acting in the spirit of faith. I told them not to worry. I definitely felt guided from above—as I left my apartment, I noticed my hall light flickering.

Part Two

HOPE

Chapter 20

As I boarded the airplane, I felt good about the last few weeks. I knew I would do my best to make a difference in someone's life. As the plane started rising up into the sky, I opened my devotional and read: "You do not need to see far ahead. Just one step at a time. The same light to guide you as the Host of Heavens know. Only self can cast a shadow on the way."

I knew I wouldn't be arriving in Rome for fifteen hours, and with the time change, I would need to be awake and refreshed for a full day of researching my heir apparent. Shiloh was sound asleep in his carrier, and because I had no one occupying the seat next to me, I took advantage of my laptop and started mapping out my steps once I touched Italian soil. I had been given a great deal of information by Dr. G., but names and addresses didn't mean much if I didn't know the basic surroundings and what to expect. I was fortunate that I had a plug for my computer—a rarity on most planes.

About halfway into my flight, I was awakened by a nice-looking, older gentleman who offered to buy me a drink. His accent was very European, and I was hoping it was Italian. After all, I needed all the help I could get with my upcoming mission.

"Am I to assume you are American, *signorina?*" he asked with a wink.

"Hello. Yes, I am American. And I would love a glass of wine. Is Rome your home?" I asked, with a hopeful voice.

"Ah, yes. Let me order us both a glass of wine. Perhaps I might sit next to you for a short while, *si?*" he asked and sat without waiting for my answer.

As we visited over our wine, I was thrilled to find he owned a small shop of religious items across from the courtyard of St. Peter's Basilica. He gave me the name in Italian: *Angelo di Luce.* I attempted to remember the name, but finally I asked for the English translation to keep from forgetting it. When I learned what it meant in English, I knew I would be hard pressed to forget such a beautiful name—it also took on a deeper meaning. *Angel of Light* would be one of my first shops to explore when I get to Rome.

CHAPTER 21

THE REMAINDER OF THE trip was uneventful. The flight attendants were very nice and allowed Shiloh up on my lap and under my blanket for many hours. They took turns holding and cuddling him in the empty seat next to me. He was actually no extra work, and I was pleased all went as planned. The shop owner handed me his business card as we deplaned, and I felt good that I already knew one person in Rome. This fact seemed to put me at ease, but in the back of my mind, I kept hearing Mandie's voice telling me to never let my guard down.

I was able to spot my raspberry-colored luggage right away, and I was able to find my way outside the airport in a matter of minutes. I whispered a prayer asking for guidance to spot a reputable taxi driver, and the prayer was answered immediately when a young man approached me with a smile. He actually reminded me of Michael, so perhaps that was my sign. Of course, I knew that Shiloh would be the determining factor, and I reached into his cage to bring him out into the Rome sunshine.

"Hello, *signorina* and little *cucciolo*," he said, reaching to touch the little guy's head.

"Hello," I said. "this is Shiloh. My name is Carrie. Do you speak English?"

"Yes, I do. My name is Affonso. May I drive you anywhere special?" he asked, giving me great eye contact.

"Well, I'm not sure. Are you a dog lover?" I asked with a tease in my voice.

"*Sì*," he answered, while reaching for Shiloh.

I wasn't sure what I expected, but I certainly didn't expect what happened next. Affonso reached into my arms, pulled the little guy out of my grasp, and started talking softly as he cuddled him in his arms. The true surprise was Shiloh letting all of it happen. No growling, no barking, no whining—only pure contentment.

The start of my Rome adventure began that very moment. I asked Affonso for recommendations on B and Bs, and he drove me to Domus Betti. It was the perfect place to call home: just outside the Vatican walls and in the middle of the exclusive Prati district. Affonso told me it was managed by the owner, and he mentioned that small pets were welcome free of charge. With Shiloh willingly permitted and a free breakfast, what more could a gal ask?

Chapter 22

WHAT A LOVELY B and B. It had all the comforts of home without being glitzy—a modest, single bed with a rattan dresser, desk, and love seat. The elongated window overlooked a small, private garden, giving me a sense of security yet some access to nature. Orchids, lilies, and roses were abundant and nestled alongside vegetables and herbs. The aroma, when my window was open, reminded me of my grandmother's perfume. And unlike in the states, no screens were covering the outside world. Dr. Gabel would definitely approve of my new surroundings.

I was pleased to find Internet access, and I placed my laptop on the small desk to be used once I emptied my suitcase. Several hangers in the freestanding bamboo closet allowed me to unpack with little effort, and I actually felt good about my new home away from home. Shiloh immediately found the wide-window ledge, and he was intrigued by all the bird noise and the slight breeze blowing his ears away from his face. *Thank you, God, for allowing me to find this glorious bungalow.*

I knew the first thing I needed to do was e-mail both Michael and Mandie to let them know I arrived safely and tell them my new address. Once I got the basics out of the way, I could concentrate on finding Angelo Giovanni. I opened the portfolio Dr. Gabel had given me, and I found where he spent a great deal of his time. Given the time of day, I decided to start my conquest in the morning and attempt to shake off the jet lag, which seemed to be settling into my being. Funny that I wasn't yet hungry—at least not *restaurant* hungry. I grabbed my protein bar and settled in on top of the bedspread as Shiloh curled at my feet. I can remember thinking, *I will just rest my eyes for a short while.*

It didn't surprise me to find I had actually slept until the wee hours of the morning. I was wide awake, so I walked over to close my window (the night air was a bit cool) and turned on my desk lamp. I reached for one of my bottles of water, and I sat down to set a course of action for the morning.

I was always one to leave myself notes, and I knew that I needed more than notes for the upcoming job. I quickly typed out a brief outline.

I'm not sure why, but my mind drifted off to Michael. I decided to e-mail my thoughts to him:

"Hey there! Can't sleep. Rome is beautiful, and so is my small but quaint B and B. Tomorrow, I will attempt to run into our heir apparent. Should find him one of two places. Hopefully he's a good guy. Shiloh is well and doesn't seem homesick yet. I'll keep you updated. Carrie."

CHAPTER 23

I AWOKE, ONCE AGAIN, to sunshine in my eyes. It took me a second or two to remember where I was, and when it occurred to me, a smile came over my face. In no time, I was dressed and opened the window to listen to birds and catch a light breeze. Shiloh found his way to his new favorite spot, and he kept watch on the window ledge. It didn't take me long to remember that the Domas Betti offered a free breakfast, and I felt bad having to close the window on Shiloh while I quickly slipped out of my room.

"I'll be right back, little guy," I said, in a soothing tone.

What an adorable breakfast area, I thought as I walked into a colorfully painted room with fresh flowers and fruit on each table. For some reason, I ate more than I normally would. *Who's kidding who?* I thought. I hadn't really had a full meal since the plane, and that wasn't really filling. I grabbed a free bottle of water and headed back to the room.

"So, Shiloh, are you ready to walk the streets of Rome?" I asked with a smile on my face. He definitely intuited what I meant because he headed for his lead and sat waiting for me to connect it. I grabbed a couple of pages of notes, my pink baseball hat with the star of the Dallas Cowboys on the front, my satchel with my camera, and my sun wear and sweater. We were off!

It wasn't as early as I would have wanted, but eleven o'clock in the morning was the perfect time of day to blend in with vacationers. Both old and young were everywhere, and each and every person we passed smiled and looked down at the *cucciolo* by my side. Funny how, no matter how old a dog is, if it's small enough, everyone calls it a puppy.

Within minutes, we were able to enter the walls of the holy city state that houses the Catholic Church. The portfolio was specific as to where Angelo would be working as a tour guide. I even had his picture with me in case I got overwhelmed and couldn't differentiate between the Italian men. It didn't take me long to notice that all men in Italy gave me extremely good eye contact as I walked by—and I could see how one might get caught up in the flirting game.

I told myself that I might not find Angelo for several days if he was a guide and off with a paying client or two. Given that fact, I started noticing my surroundings. I was in awe of the beauty of St. Peter's Square. My eyes immediately noticed the colorful uniforms of the Swiss guards, and I heard other Americans saying that they were originally designed by Michelangelo. *Oh my gosh, the history here in Rome is so different from the states,* I thought. I could already see how the people of Italy left everything as it was centuries before … nothing had been torn down. I found myself stepping over pillars that fell hundreds of years before with walkways blended around them.

I soon found myself walking in the same courtyard where the Pope, back in the early 80s, had an attempt made on his life. Masses of people were pointing to a middle balcony of St. Peter's Basilica where the Pope would appear and give his blessing. It didn't take me long to get caught up in how special Rome truly was. I constantly had to tell myself to focus and continue looking for Angelo. Perhaps he didn't start his day particularly early. I did have one other place I could look for him, though.

CHAPTER 24

I TOOK OUT MY map of the city, and the two of us started walking to Petrocchi, a well-known Italian shoe shop for high-profile people looking for both made-to-order and ready-made shoes. It wasn't long before I knew it was going to be too much for Shiloh. By noon, the temperatures were in the 80s, and I found myself stopping every other block and giving him some of my bottled water.

I had just finished rationalizing my predicament when I saw a scooter rental stand. I soon found the only scooter with a front basket, paid, and set out again. This was the way to see Rome! I passed so many restaurants with such inviting names, such as *Sabatini* and *Tuscolo,* and I finally saw the shop where I was hoping to find Angelo. I knew most of the shops in Rome were open mornings until 1 p.m., and I also knew they would reopen after about 4 p.m. I arrived just in time to catch Angelo as he was getting off work—if he was there.

I parked the scooter, grabbed Shiloh, and headed into the shop. My eyes soon found my way to a tall, dark-haired, young man helping two middle-aged women. One look told me they had been there awhile—they had shoes and boxes surrounding their feet. I needed to get closer to make sure he was the subject of my portfolio. As I got within thirty feet, Shiloh unexpectedly jumped out of my arms and headed down the aisle toward the shoppers.

My reaction was to start calling out Shiloh's name over and over until I suddenly saw him reach the group of three and sit down in front of the young man. As I approached—apologizing for the inconvenience—I knew my red face proved how embarrassed I was. It didn't take me long to look into Angelo's eyes and know I was at the right shop. I was further flustered by the fact that he was now holding my dog.

"Sir, I am so sorry for my dog's actions," I said. I meant every word.

"No need to worry, Miss. You have a very spirited puppy," Angelo said with a smile.

As I reached for my dog, I noticed Angelo's eyes looking down to view my tennis shoes. This was the first time the thought hit me: I was in a shoe store, and I was supposed to be looking to buy a pair of shoes—expensive, Italian shoes.

"Ah, don't mind me," I said, "I'll just start looking by myself. When you have completed your transactions, I'll be ready to be helped."

As I walked away, whispering to Shiloh, I found my stomach topsy-turvy for the first time since I had touched Italian soil. It was becoming increasingly clear to me now. This was my only purpose in flying to Europe. I would be sole determiner as to whether Angelo would receive a gift to turn his world upside down.

CHAPTER 25

I T REALLY WASN'T SO far-fetched. I found myself longing for a pair of classy, handmade, Italian shoes. Angelo was right, however, when he eyed my sneakers and wondered what on earth I was doing in such a high-end establishment. I smiled to myself thinking how observant he was upon first meeting me. Still, there would be no way he would find out I couldn't afford any shoes in the store. If he allowed people to assume he was the owner, I could definitely pull off being a woman of means.

I already had spotted a beautiful pair of handmade sandals, so I was ready when he walked up and saw them in my hands.

"Miss, are you ready for me to help you?" he asked in strained English.

"Actually," I said, "I'm not sure if you can fit my narrow foot."

"Most all of our shoes are quite a bit narrower than American-made shoes," he answered.

This wouldn't be as easy as I initially thought. Putting down Shiloh, I held up the sandals and asked what colors they came in.

"Any color you would like, Miss," he said, as if teasing me.

"Perhaps brown or tan," I answered, "I am new to Rome and would like to see quite a few of your sights. I'm thinking sandals might be good for all the walking I will need to do, no?"

"No," he answered, "if you want to see the sites, I would recommend a good tour guide—not walking around by yourself with your little puppy."

Perfect, I thought, *Could this be working out any better?*

"That had not occurred to me," I said convincingly, "Perhaps I need a guide more than I need a new pair of sandals. Would you be able to direct me to a reputable one in the Vatican area?"

"There are several good guides, but only one *great* guide," he added with authority.

"Okay, I'll bite. Can you direct me to the *great* guide?" By this time, I had started to laugh out loud.

"Yes. My name is Angelo, and it would be a pleasure to be your *great* guide."

"My name is Jeanne, and I would love to hire you as my *great* guide. You do surprise me, however, because I thought you owned this shoe store ... no?"

Angelo's voice got low as he said, "I only work here mornings. My love is touring beautiful American girls, such as yourself. Are you free to start today?"

"Actually," I said, "I'm free this very minute."

CHAPTER 26

MANDIE CERTAINLY WOULDN'T HAVE believed I was on a scooter sitting behind Angelo with Shiloh's ears wagging in the wind. But then again, she wouldn't have believed I would have been so bold to fly half way around the world after answering a want ad in the paper either. It bothered me just a little when Angelo seemed way too eager to take an American girl around Rome, but perhaps I was looking for some sign other than honesty. I wanted to believe he was like the person represented in the portfolio. I would feel quite a bit safer knowing he was one of the good guys. But until I confirmed that very fact, I had no intention of letting my guard down.

"I would love to see the Colosseum," I shouted into Angelo's ear as we rounded a corner.

"I would love to show you the Colosseum," he answered, "We should be there in just a few minutes. Have you seen any sites yet?"

"Not really," I assured him. "Where would I have found you to take me around normally?"

"My corner is right across from St. Peter's Square, and I would have found you first," he said with a chuckle in his voice.

At least he was telling the truth according to the information I had on him. I would really have to challenge Angelo as the day progressed. It would be hard remembering the name Dr. Gabel gave me. Please, dear Lord, help me respond to the name *Jeanne*.

It didn't take long before I found myself in awe of the enormous sight before us. As Angelo turned the scooter into a small parking area, I couldn't help but think I had gone back in time. Roman time.

"Can we walk in and around the Colosseum?" I asked, eyes attempting to take in as much of the unbelievable structure as possible.

"Of course we can," Angelo answered, "Bring your puppy, and let me start doing my job."

Even if I hadn't been on a chosen course of action, I would have found my new tour guide charming and informative. We walked around and through history for what seemed like hours. He let me stop and take pictures and never once checked his watch. I was awestruck with the massive structure that had survived time. I actually had to push myself into asking questions not relevant to the Colosseum.

"How does one become a tour guide in Rome?" I asked, hoping for some of his personal life to unfold.

"It is what it is," he said as he looked off into the distance.

I sensed some sadness in his world, but it would take more than one day for him to trust and confide in me. I knew my greatest gift was my ability to read people and their emotions; I knew timing was everything; and I knew it was not the time to quiz Angelo on the look in his eyes.

CHAPTER 27

B Y THE TIME I had returned the scooter and walked back to my B and B, the sun was just going down. Shiloh didn't even bother to find his way to the window ledge. He drank from his water dish and cuddled up at the foot of the bed. I knew just how he felt. I knew I would not be dining out. I certainly would not be taking that short walk down the banks of the river Tiber into the medieval district of Trastevere (even though it was at the top of my list). I knew it was a popular nightspot for locals and tourists alike, but it would have to wait another day.

As I took off my baseball hat and let my hair fall down, I felt my body start to unwind and headed into the tub. A long, hot bath was just what I needed. It would be the perfect time to think about the day and contemplate what the next day would hold. As I reached for the light switch, the ceiling light went on and off—and then I was left in total darkness. I had to grab a candle from my dresser along with my devotional to see what the powers that be were trying to tell me.

"You must trust me wholly. This lesson has to be learned. You shall be helped, you shall be led, guided, continually. Trust My tender love. You have much to learn at turning out fear and being at peace. You must not doubt."

A cup of tea and hot bath were all I needed. I walked over to my computer with the aim of telling Michael I had a productive day.

"Hey There! Yet another day in lovely Roma. You'd be proud of me … I met Angelo and actually paid him for touring services. And I almost bought a pair of sandals from the elite shop where he works part-time. Haven't decided yet if he's a good guy. Can confirm something in his past makes him sad. Plan is to literally tail him tomorrow and check out his day-to-day happenings before I hire him full-time. Thus far, I haven't needed to establish a cover. Hope Missy and you are both fine. No, I'm not missing American food. I am, however, starting to miss your smile. Later, Carrie."

After I opened the window to hear the breeze and smell the roses, I slept like a baby. The private garden somehow gave me comfort, and Shiloh gave me all I needed to settle in. The powers that be were telling me to trust. *Okay, trust it is.*

CHAPTER 28

I SLEPT IN FOR the second day in a row. As I rolled over on top of Shiloh, the phone next to the bed started ringing. By the fourth ring, I came to my senses.

"Hello," I said sleepily.

"Hello, Carrie. This is Dr. Gabel. I hope I didn't awaken you."

"Oh, hello, Doctor. I was just thinking about getting up when the phone rang. It's so good to hear from you," I said as I sat up, feet draped over the side of the bed.

"I take it you find everything at your B and B to your liking?" he asked.

"That seems to tell me you played a part in where I am staying. How did you pull that one off?" I said quizzically.

"When one has lived as long as I have lived—and traveled to as many places as I have traveled—choosing the perfect B and B was not so extraordinary," he answered. "I have many homes, and I move around quite often."

"Just so I understand: you hired the taxi driver to find me and recommend this great place?" I questioned, knowing his answer.

"Let me just say that I knew the Domas would be ideal for the two of you. Now, then, have you been able to locate our Mr. Giovanni?" he asked.

"Yes, Doctor, I have. I feel it went very well. I spent the afternoon touring with him yesterday, and I intend to verify the information you shared with me in his portfolio today," I countered.

"Excellent," Dr. Gabel answered with delayed speech and a sudden coughing attack. "Carry on, then, Miss Carrie, and I will speak with you in a few days. Take care and please remember: things are not always as they seem."

As I hung the receiver up, chills went up and down my arms. It was a good thing Dr. Gabel called because I was starting to think of the trip as a vacation instead of a serious undercover mission. Today would take some planning on my part. I went to my carry-on bag and pulled out two different wigs. I shook out the short, blond hair. A miniskirt, net hose, high heels, and a frilly blouse would make up my outfit for the day. I could start to envision my transformation. If Angelo had anything to hide, perhaps he would reveal it shortly.

It didn't take me long to shower, dress, eat, and leave Shiloh watching the birds on his usual ledge. I had called the number on the taxi driver's business card the night before and left a message. I said I needed his services for the entire day. As I walked up to his Audi, I could see he did not recognize me. My confidence level rose knowing my disguise was convincing.

Once I confirmed I was the one who had contacted him, we were off. At least I felt secure with Affonso, knowing that Dr. Gabel had made the initial arrangements with him. I shared that I was researching lifestyles of Italian men and that we would need to be discreet. He did not seem to have a problem with me being his day fare, and I requested that he make the drive over to Angelo's shoe shop.

As we pulled up across from the shop, I could see much activity inside. I immediately found Angelo in my vision and made mention who I was watching. As we sat in the morning sunshine, I pulled out two croissants and handed one to Affonso.

"I'm hoping our day is very boring," I said, eyes watching the store front.

"I'm hoping your wish is confirmed," Affonso answered.

It took about an hour before I noticed my heir apparent exiting the side door of the shoe shop. He walked directly to a small car parked about a half block down and headed out into the streets of Rome. I assured Affonso there would be a bonus at the end of the day if he made sure we tailed him without being noticed.

Winding in and around the narrow streets, we soon came to a Western Union Quick Cash. I knew I was risking him recognizing me in such a small setting, but I needed to go inside to see what he was doing. I asked Affonso to go in with me and pretend we were a couple. I actually grabbed his hand as we walked in the door of the small building. Once inside, I noticed Angelo in line. It looked as though he were going to buy a Western Union MoneyGram. I took out a map of Rome and motioned to Affonso to study it with me to draw less attention to both of us. As we stood in one corner of the small room, Angelo took money out of his pocket. I watched as he counted out ten hundred dollar bills. American dollar bills. *Who on earth could he be sending that much money to?* As he finished filling out the paperwork and walked away from the counter, I watched as he crumpled up a copy of his transaction and threw it in a wastebasket next to the door.

My legs were moving long before I thought to tell Affonso what I was up to. As I reached into the container, I pulled the pink, wrinkled paper out. I was placing it in my purse at the same time I was heading out the door to see where Angelo was off to. He was already in his car and driving before we both reached the taxi.

"Don't lose him!" I shouted.

Thank goodness American rules of the road didn't seem to apply in Rome. Our car was zigzagging in and out of traffic seconds after the key hit the ignition. I felt as though we were in a reenactment of the movie *Bullitt* with Steve McQueen. The movie in my head made the experience seem almost surreal as we darted around cars, buses, and little, old ladies walking their dogs.

"Oh my gosh, why is he driving so fast?" I said while strapping my seat belt tighter.

"Hopefully it is not because he knows we are following him," he answered.

That thought never occurred to me. *How could he know we were tailing him? Not a chance! I've been too careful in my disguise. He was already out the door before I reached into the trash can. He would have no idea who owned the car we were in, so certainly he couldn't recognize it.* It was almost as if he routinely covered his tracks—as if he normally made sure he wasn't being followed. As if he had something to hide.

"Gone. He has disappeared. I've lost him," Affonso said with certainty as we slowed down to a crawl. "I am so sorry, Miss. I have no idea how he got away. I will not be requesting the bonus you promised."

Chapter 29

It was long past the time to catch Angelo back at the shoe store. I asked to be taken to the Vatican area on the chance I could spot him before he found a willing tourist. As we sat in the taxi, eyes looking toward Angelo's corner, I suddenly remembered I had tucked the copy of the money order in my purse. I unfolded it and recognized only his name. He had not entered a street address, only a local post office box. No phone number. The amount of $1,000 stood out on the far right of the page. He was sending it to S. Bryant at another anonymous post office box. No phone number. Capri. That was it. Simple and concise and it left me bewildered.

After another hour had gone by, I requested to be taken back to my B and B. *So much for acquiring any more knowledge on my new best friend, Angelo.* I was pretty down, and evidently it showed on my face. Affonso was turning the car around, and I noticed him looking at me from the rearview mirror.

"Miss Carrie," he said, getting my attention, "would you like me to accompany you out to a real Italian dinner this evening? A pretty girl like you should not hide away surrounded by walls while in Rome."

CHAPTER 30

HAVING A DOG AROUND confirmed the statement I had heard years before. Dogs always greeted you with unconditional love. I certainly needed that love as I walked into my bungalow. Shiloh's tail never stopped wagging, and he allowed me to cuddle him on the bed for several minutes. I was just plain tired, and laying on top of my bed allowed me to slowly unwind. As I was taking off my blond wig, I heard my computer acknowledge a new e-mail with a ding.

I smiled as I noticed it was from Michael. *Perfect timing. I definitely need a friend right now.*

"Hey Carrie! Good to hear from you. Both Missy and I are doing fine. We both miss your smiling face and hope you are taking everything slow and methodical. Back off and don't get involved if anything illegal is going on. I know you are there to confirm authenticity, but don't put yourself at risk. You are important to me. Take care, Michael."

Just what I needed. A reminder to stay focused, be careful, and hang in there. *I can do this. I just need a good dinner and good night's sleep. Tomorrow I can start all over again.*

It didn't take me long to shower and change before I heard a knock at my door. I was just starting to get hungry, and taking Affonso up on his dinner out seemed the perfect distraction.

"Where are we off to?" I asked.

"A very charming restaurant near the Spanish Steps," he answered.

I was a little surprised to find us walking to a small, red sports car with the top down. I had to smile inside thinking about the fact that I assumed he only had a taxi to drive. *That should teach me a thing or two about assuming,* I thought.

"And just what is the name of this restaurant, my friend?" I quizzed.

"El Toula is the name. Very upscale and elegant. One to suit the needs of a very beautiful American woman."

It took no time at all, and I was actually a little sad we arrived at our destination so fast. The wind blowing through my hair and the night air was absolutely divine.

As we walked inside, I noticed vaulted ceilings, large archways, and a charming bar area. Our table overlooked the Spanish Steps with fewer tourists on them as night started approaching. Affonso ordered wine from quite an extensive and varied list.

"I am so appreciative you extended me an invitation to this lovely restaurant," I said with a broad smile.

"It is my pleasure, Miss Carrie. Our menu has one section devoted to Venetian specialties, in honor of the restaurant's origins. I would suggest beginning with a bowl of linguine with lobster, cherry tomatoes, and sweet red pepper. We could then enjoy their potato dumplings with basil-laced pesto and prawns. Of course, to finish off our evening, we must have their chocolate parfait with vanilla sauce and hazelnut ice cream."

"Order away," I said as my eyes drank in my surroundings.

As we enjoyed our second glass of wine and my body seemed to relax enough to enjoy Roman time, I noticed couple after couple with arms around each other. Their eyes were not wandering, and their smiles were expressive and sincere. This would definitely be a place to return to with a loved one.

The threesome next to our table was dining on fresh asparagus and black truffles. Their conversation seemed to tell a story reminiscent of *The Thorn Birds* starring Richard Chamberlain. The only woman at the table asked the young seminarian if he loved her daughter. He replied, "Yes." She then asked if her daughter loved him. Again, he replied, "Yes." Even though I felt I was overhearing a very private confession, I could not break my concentration until I heard her final question. She said, "Why on earth are you studying for the priesthood here in Rome?"

"Is anything wrong, Miss Carrie?" asked Affonso.

"No, I am so sorry. My mind wandered, and I apologize for not being more attentive."

"It is all right," he answered, "When in Rome, everyone seems to be in a trance. Please enjoy your dinner and tell me how I might help you find your gentleman friend."

Chapter 31

OUR MEAL TOOK OVER two hours, and it was dark by the time Affonso was driving me back to my B and B. After a couple glasses of wine and such a wonderful dinner, I had no intention of reasoning out my next move. The night air—along with Rome's beauty—gave way to being thankful: thankful for a good-paying job, thankful for good friends back in the states, thankful for unconditional love, thankful for common sense and logic, thankful for Affonso who took me straight home.

I walked into my bungalow and was greeted by Shiloh. As I picked him up, I walked over to my devotional and sat at my desk. "Give me the gift of a brave and thankful heart. Man proves his greatness by his power to see causes for thankfulness in his life. When life seems hard, and troubles crowd, then very definitely look for causes for thankfulness. The sacrifice, the offering, is indeed a sweet incense going up to Me through the busy day."

The faith my mother instilled in me many years ago came flooding back, and I knew that a good night's sleep would put all into perspective once again. I opened my e-mail and found a recent one from Michael. I answered it with two words: "Me too."

Bed never felt so good, and with the window open, sending in a warm breeze, I slept like a baby.

CHAPTER 32

THE MORNING BROUGHT WITH it confidence and hope, and I awoke knowing how my day would be spent. After croissants and cappuccino, I pulled on my shorts, jersey racerback tank, tennis shoes, and cap and headed out the door with Shiloh leading the way. A tour of the Sistine Chapel and St. Peter's sounded like the perfect start to any day. And I knew a great tour guide.

I spotted Angelo from half a block away. Since he was used to searching for tourists, it didn't surprise me when he started waving at us. I returned the wave, and I couldn't help but put a smile on my face as we approached. Shiloh had already picked him out and acknowledged with tail wagging and a low, whining sound.

"How is the American girl and her *cucciolo?*" he asked, returning my smile.

"We are just fine, and we're hoping for a tour of St. Peter's today?" I questioned.

"St. Peter's it is!" he acknowledged as he picked up Shiloh.

Today will be my day to find out more personal information on my heir apparent. We walked side by side, and Angelo started telling me the most remarkable facts about Rome. Tourists and guides were everywhere, but I felt that Angelo's attention to detail far surpassed any other details I overheard.

St. Peter's Basilica was absolutely breathtaking. I could not help but look up and all around. Over forty separate altars with every inch carved out of marble or bronze. As we approached Michelangelo's "Pieta," Angelo explained the marble sculpture was made for a French cardinal's funeral monument, but it was moved to this first chapel on the right as we entered the church. Hard to believe the artist was only twenty-two years old when he created such an intense piece.

"He was so young," I stated. "How old are you, Angelo?"

"I am twenty-six years old," he said.

"You never did tell me what brought you to Rome," I said.

"I was very good in school, and I learned English quickly. It was suggested I go to Rome to take people on tours."

"Who suggested?" I asked.

"My family," he said with a pause in his voice.

The one thing I knew about people was when they were not telling the truth. Considering how uncomfortable Angelo had just become, I knew, without a doubt, that he was hiding something. I also knew I needed to seem more interested in my tour than his personal life.

We continued walking on our tour, and we found our way to the statue of St. Peter. The custom, Angelo stated, was to kiss his right foot. As I neared, I could see it had been kissed smooth.

We soon found ourselves looking at a beautiful altar designed by Bernini back in the seventeenth century. Looking up, we saw a bronze canopy. Above that, we saw a cupola designed by Michelangelo. My tour guide was excellent at providing factual information, and I secretly thanked Dr. Gabel for this chance of a lifetime.

As we walked to the Sistine Chapel from St. Peter's, Angelo let me look into the pope's private garden. Lush greenery was everywhere, and I could feel the tranquility it surely brought to the head of the Catholic Church.

I felt as though I were but a small dwarf in a huge castle, and I found myself walking slowly and looking up constantly. I heard Angelo describing the pope's crypt where 70 percent of all popes had been buried and a gilded, bronze sunburst holding a symbolic dove. I felt Angelo's hand as he guided me. *What a sensitive person he is,* I thought. I wanted to believe he was on the up and up, but I still needed confirmation.

As we were walking through a museum (en route to the Sistine Chapel) containing art and objects from the world's major countries, I took another shot at finding out just who my heir apparent truly was.

"Angelo, you seem to know so much. How long have you been touring the multitudes here in Rome?"

"About eight years now," he answered as we rounded yet another hallway.

"Wow," I said, "I would think you would have enough savings to buy your own house by now. Do you own one?"

"No, Miss," he said, looking downward, "I save all my money for something other than material gain for myself."

"Oh," I said innocently, "are you able to put your hard-earned money into a savings of some sort?"

"One might say I invest my earnings for a great deal of profit."

"That sounds like something I need to check into. Any chance I can get an inside scoop on your investments?" I asked.

"There is a great deal of risk in what I invest in—as well as danger. You do not want to know anything about my business dealings," he said with both hands on my shoulders.

"Now you're scaring me, Angelo," I said. I could not help but think drugs might be involved. "Is what you do legal?" I asked with a pleading tone in my voice.

"Let it suffice for me to simply say that I do what I need to do."

CHAPTER 33

A s we finally entered the Sistine Chapel, the beauty was almost overwhelming. Both walls were painted by famous artists, and my eyes scanned "The Crossing of the Red Sea," "The Sermon on the Mount," and "The Last Supper." Angelo told me to look upward, and the ceiling painted by Michelangelo was breathtaking. Four and a half years he worked, following the progression taken from the *Old Testament*. As I studied The Separation of Light from Darkness, The Creation of Adam, and Expulsion from the Garden of Eden, my mind was overcome with the enormity of his project.

"Do you not feel blessed every day you see this, Angelo?" I asked.

"Yes, I do."

"Thank you so much for taking the time out of your day to bring me to this wonderful place," I said with sincerity, "I feel as though my life is complete now."

"I am so happy you feel that way, but please don't think this is the only beauty in Rome," Angelo said, "There is so much more to show you—and after all, it is my job."

"Yes, that is true. But you have such dedication to your profession that I feel like it is not work for you," I said. "I do have more I would like to see, so let's discuss my wants once we find our way outside."

We soon followed the crowds outside and into the sunlight. Shiloh was able to move his little legs once again. Angelo found us a grassy knoll, and we settled in (allowing me to bring out a map of the surrounding regions, away from the city of Rome itself).

"I so enjoy this city, but I also will need your help to explore other areas," I said.

"What is it that you would like me to show you?" Angelo asked.

"I am a teacher of tennis in the States, and I would like to explore the several resorts in and around Rome. I will need to inquire about their facilities and if they would have any openings for a pro," I said.

I hoped my lie came out convincingly because I was actually surprised when I said it. I knew I had planned on saying it, but I wasn't sure how it sounded until I heard it with my own ears.

"I will have no problem taking you around during the week on any day but Wednesday. I have another commitment on that day, but I'm certain we can work around it," Angelo said. His eyes were drifting downward again, and I had that same uneasy feeling that he was hiding something.

"I certainly do not want to take all of your time," I said, "I will simply take that day to sightsee on my own." My mind had already started to think about the particulars of tailing Angelo once again. At least I knew what day I would need Affonso and his taxi. It took me just a second to realize that the next day *was* Wednesday.

"It sounds like we will start traveling to our resorts the day after tomorrow," I said. "Right?"

"That is right," Angelo said, "I will meet you here about ten o'clock on Thursday morning."

As we parted, I could not help but think how much I wanted Angelo to be one of the good guys in my world.

CHAPTER 34

As Shiloh and I walked back to our B and B, I found myself starting to get really hungry. It had been a while since the croissant. It was the time of day that I usually missed my close friends—the kind you can call up and ask to meet you at a restaurant. I'd just have to look for some place with tables outside so I could include the little guy in the mix. It only took another block before my eyes spotted *La Pizzeria*. A group of Americans with UCLA sweatshirts were laughing outside and toasting their wine glasses to some recent happening. Of course, the moment they spotted my Dallas Cowboys cap and Shiloh in my arms, they motioned for me to join them. It seemed as if I were instantly included in their reunion party, and a cheer rose loudly into the warm night air when they discovered I was from Texas.

The good thing about pizza is that it fills you up quickly and leaves plenty of room for wine. I definitely needed the spontaneity of the moment, and I passed Shiloh freely around to each college student. We discussed the popular nightspots, tourist attractions, museums, churches, and places to stand for great pictures. The conversation was light and lively—perfect to keep me from thinking about what my day would be like when I awoke in the morning. After exchanging e-mail addresses and far too many digital pictures, Shiloh and I were off once again to our secluded garden apartment.

It was just a short walk home, and I was exhausted. My routine over the past few days had been to unlock my door, open the window in my bungalow, and place Shiloh on his favorite ledge. And then I usually walked over to my desk to check for e-mails. There was just one from Michael, and I couldn't help but laugh as I read it.

"Hey there! Missy has now officially become my cat. She asked me yesterday if she could come over to my apartment and visit, and she hasn't moved from the couch yet. She definitely has those 'missing you' blues. Of course, she really makes it hard for me to not have the same problem. Issues of abandonment are filtering into both of our lives now. Let me say it just one more time … you are missed! Michael P. S. Take care of yourself."

I turned off my computer, reached for the light switch, and made a giant leap onto the bed. I was able to convince myself I could sleep with my clothes on, and in no time, I was looking at the shadows on the ceiling. Angelo seemed like such a nice young man. What on earth could be so important for him to risk bringing danger into his world? Why would he be sending such a large sum of money to a post office box? What did he do every Wednesday that was so serious he couldn't take around a paying customer? I was starting to wonder whether my vision was clouded, whether I was not seeing the whole picture.

These questions—and many more—should be answered when I am not so tired, I thought. As the breeze entered into the room and Shiloh cuddled up at my feet, I knew what I needed to do in the morning.

CHAPTER 35

T HE SOUND OF BIRDS chirping actually had me thinking I was dreaming. Once I heard Shiloh's low growling, I knew exactly where I was, and I knew he was watching another small animal from the window ledge.

"Hey, leave the wildlife alone and come over here," I said, still drowsy.

I reached over for the phone and called the number on Affonso's business card. After setting up a ten o'clock pickup time, I laid there thinking about my strategy for the day. Yet another Wednesday in Rome, and once again, I needed to change identities and put on another one of my wigs. Altering my appearance had become quite a challenge because I normally wore very little makeup and extremely casual clothing. My mind drifted to what I had packed before leaving Texas, and I pictured my outfit for the day.

"Okay, little guy, I have to get showered first, and then we'll go for a walk."

We were soon heading out the door. I had a cappuccino in one hand and leash in the other. I couldn't decide whether I loved Rome best in the early mornings or after dark with the lights of the city. At this time, there was definitely not as much rushing around as in the States, and watching storekeepers sweep their areas clean (as pigeons attempted to pick up the leftovers) was a sight I hadn't witnessed before. A brisk, hour-long walk got my thought waves working, and I was actually looking forward to the day ahead.

I knew Affonso, once again, would be surprised to see me walk out of my bungalow apartment. As I opened my front door, I could see the astonishment in his eyes. Bright red wig, leopard hoodie, black miniskirt, and mesh hose just about said it all. I wanted to become someone completely different, and it seemed like I succeeded.

"Hey, Affonso, how's your morning going?" I asked.

"Is that you, Miss Carrie?"

"Yes, it sure is. I'm ready for our day together," I answered.

As he opened the back taxi door, I corrected him and nodded to the front seat. Because I wasn't sure how much time we would be spending together, I didn't want him to watch what I was saying through the rearview mirror. Besides, Affonso was soon becoming a friend—not simply a driver.

"Where to?" he asked.

"Back to the original shoe shop we drove to last week," I answered.

As we started on our way, I pulled out a couple croissants and handed one to Affonso. His smile put us both at ease, and it didn't take long before we were discussing the small cars of Italy as well as random thoughts on the state of the economy.

"Pull over here," I said as I motioned to a space overlooking the side alley and front window of the shop. "We now wait for any activity."

After a couple hours, I was beginning to think Angelo might only sell shoes that day. I had just turned my head to the side when Affonso put his hand on my chin and directed my attention to the alley. I didn't want to believe it, but sure enough, Angelo was walking to another small car. This car was not the same one from the last outing, and that puzzled me as much as the fact that he darted out of the shop in record time.

"Here we go again," I said. "We can't lose him, so stay close."

Staying close was only the beginning of our problems. As we waited for Angelo to, once again, back out of the alley, he surprised us both by heading to the rear of the shop. I had assumed there was only parking in the rear, but within seconds, it occurred to me that there must also be an exit.

"Quick," I yelled, "head down the alley! We can't lose him!"

In the short time it took us to reach the back, he had disappeared. My head moved back and forth frantically before I spotted him out of the corner of my eye. He had actually driven over someone's backyard, and he was heading south down some narrow street.

"There he is," I said, pointing toward where I spotted his car. "Do whatever it takes, Affonso, we need to catch up with him."

You'd have thought I offered a king's ransom the way he turned the wheel sharply and headed over some poor Italian's backyard and garden area. *Oh my gosh, such beautiful flowers and we just drove right over them!* As I was tightening my seat belt, I found we were actually catching up to Angelo's small blue car. *Surely, he didn't think he was being followed?* I thought. As that thought hit me, yet another came into my mind: *Perhaps he is just making sure he isn't followed.*

"We have him now, Miss Carrie. I promise you, we will not lose him."

It seemed like an eternity of winding in and around Rome before we finally spotted yet another Western Union Quick Cash. Angelo's car pulled up directly in front of it, and he jumped out. We double parked in front of another taxi, and I grabbed Affonso's hand as we entered into quite a large sub-station. This particular one had three different lines, and I immediately found Angelo standing behind the shortest.

As he approached the attendant, he once again took money out of his pocket and counted ten hundred dollar bills. American dollar bills. It had only been one week, and he was already sending more money to someone—a great deal of money to someone. After he finished filling out the paperwork, he crumpled his copy and tossed it at a wastebasket as he headed out the front door. He missed, and I nonchalantly picked up the pink paper. I acted like I was placing it into the trash. We were back outside within a few seconds and walking to our taxi. I looked around. There was no sign of Angelo.

CHAPTER 36

I WAS FEELING PRETTY down. It sounded simple when Dr. Gabel asked me to verify that Angelo was honorable enough to accept some special gift he wanted to hand over. *Honorable* did not seem to be the adjective that came to mind.

"Where to now?" Affonso asked.

"Let's go to the place that I hope will bring me some comfort and peace. I met a gentleman on the plane who told me he owned a store not far from the Vatican. The name is *Angel of Light* in English. It sounds like a good place for me to shop for some of my favorite loves. Can you please help me find his store?" I asked.

"I know just the place," Affonso said as he started the car.

Slowly winding in and around the narrow streets of Rome seemed to bring a calm to my spirit, and I reached into my purse for my daily devotional. The crumpled pink piece of paper jumped out at me. There it was again: the same large dollar amount, the same post office box in Capri. Another thousand dollars being sent out of Rome to S. Bryant. It had all gotten my attention, and I intended to unwind the mystery.

"There it is: the storefront with the big angel standing by the door," Affonso stated as he pointed his finger about half a block down.

Good, I thought, *At least not everyone is hiding something. At least the Italian gentleman on the plane was telling the truth about his shop.* I started getting excited about the possibility of taking a special angel from Rome back to the States with me.

"I'm not far from my bungalow now, Affonso. You can drop me off, and I'll walk home from here. Thank you for all your effort today. I'll call you soon."

As his car drove away, the thought hit me: *Oh my gosh, I'm still in my red wig, miniskirt, and mesh hose. The owner would never identify me as the young lady he met on the airplane. Oh well,* I thought, *I'm in this for the long haul, so I guess I'll just have to go in and shop as is.*

As I entered the shop, I became completely entranced by the religious objects on every table and wall—and even hanging from the ceiling. I had never seen so many angels of every shape and size, and I knew I would be browsing for hours. Before I could pick up the first rosary, I heard a disturbance coming from the back room. Voices seemed to be getting louder and louder, and I felt like I should disappear. I hated confrontations, and I certainly didn't want to be in the middle of one.

I walked over to quite a big bookcase and knelt down as if I were checking out book titles on the bottom row. I felt certain that, whatever the commotion, it would soon be ending. How wrong I was! Within a minute or two, several male voices entered into an area on the opposite side of the bookcase where I was kneeling. *Please, dear God, don't let them find me hiding.*

"I told you, we don't have any choice in the matter," said the first voice, almost yelling.

"And I told you, I cannot continue to pay that much money every week," said voice two.

"You think we love throwing away our hard-earned money on the threat they will do something to harm them?" asked yet another man.

"It's plain and simple: we cannot risk it. Until I come up with another plan, we must do as they request. We must make it seem as though everything is normal, and to do that, we must continue sending money every Wednesday. I am working two jobs now to add to the pool, and all of you need to do whatever it takes in order to ensure their safety," said the first voice.

Why did that first voice seem familiar? It almost sounded like Angelo, but it couldn't be. I knew God placed us in certain circumstances for a reason, but there was no way Angelo was on the other side of the bookcase. Or was he? As my heart was racing and my knees were starting to ache, the men all walked out the front door. I heard only quiet in the shop.

As I stood up, I wanted to run out the same door to get a better look at their faces. I was heading that way when I heard a woman's voice.

"May I help you with anything, Miss?" she asked.

Her sudden, soft voice startled me, and I found my mind had gone blank.

"Ah, no thanks. I was just browsing. My feet are killing me in these heels, so I think I'll come back another day," I said, hoping she bought into my explanation.

She must have because I found myself outside the shop looking around for either Angelo, his car, or any sign of a gathering of men. Nothing. The streets were clear. As I walked back to my bungalow, my mind was racing. I knew I needed to think through what had just happened.

CHAPTER 37

I couldn't get to my bungalow fast enough. I had even taken off my heels and finished walking the last block in my hose. As Shiloh greeted me, I scooped him up. We immediately ventured out into our private garden. I sat in the shade under a beautiful orange tree and opened up my devotional to read: "I lead you. The way is clear. Go forward unafraid. I am beside you. Listen, listen, listen to My voice. My hand is controlling all. Remember I can work through you better when you are at rest. Go very slowly from one duty to the next – taking time to rest and pray between. All work that results from resting with God is miracle-work."

Before I headed off to grab some much-needed sleep, my mind drifted back to the happenings of the day. Was it really possible I found my way into the one shop where Angelo was holding a meeting? I was certain that was his voice. It did almost seem too much of a coincidence—their conversation was about sending money every Wednesday. The day was Wednesday, and I had just witnessed Angelo sending one thousand dollars at a Western Union station. What were his words to me when we started touring? Something about investing his earnings for profit, something involving risk and danger.

All of it was almost too much to comprehend. Stumbling onto their conversation gave me new insight into the tightrope I was walking. That feeling of hiding behind someone's bookcase, crouched in a corner on my knees, was starting to creep into my skin. The feeling was fear. Fear of being caught. Fear I might be involved in something over my head.

As Shiloh and I headed back inside, I knew I needed to e-mail my good friends Mandie and Michael. New blood into this situation was definitely needed. As I sat down at my computer to type, the words I just read rewound over and over in my mind. *Go forward unafraid. Rest.*

Perhaps before I e-mailed anyone, I thought, I should indulge myself, soak in a warm bath and get a good night's sleep. After all, wasn't faith believing that a higher power watched out for all of us? That higher power certainly watched out for me today. Resting was something I could do. Going forward unafraid was something I would need to work on.

CHAPTER 38

AFTER SLEEPING FOR EIGHT hours, I awoke refreshed and ready for a new day. The sunshine entering into the room seemed to dance around on the bedspread, producing a rainbow of colors. As I opened the window overlooking the garden, the sweet sound of birds infiltrated my senses. *Thank you, God, for all of this beauty. Thank you for allowing me to rest. Please help me decide the next step to determine that Angelo is a deserving heir.*

And then it hit me. My mind had changed from assuming Angelo was guilty to proving he was innocent. Even though it was simply changing words around, it gave me new purpose. Up to that point, I had been taking for granted that Angelo was hiding something. Perhaps I needed to step over to his side, walk in his shoes, open my eyes, and become aware of why he did what he did. After all, I did answer an ad looking for an angel. Going over my past in accelerated motion, I found that I had always been captivated by angels. Angels were good, pure, nonjudgmental. Becoming an angel would hopefully help me enter into the world of Angelo Giovanni.

I headed over to my desk and quickly sent an e-mail to both Michael and Mandie, asking them to find out anything about the post office box on the copy of both MoneyGrams. If they could give me a lead on a physical address, I would take a day trip and check it out further. Not knowing was making my imagination run wild. I also asked them to research the name of the person the monies were being sent to.

I decided I should try to find Angelo and see whether we couldn't travel to Naples, the Mediterranean's port city. It looked like it was only a couple hours from Rome. My thoughts were interrupted by a knocking at my door. I grabbed a robe and opened it to find Angelo and two cups of cappuccino in his hands. His smile was mesmerizing, and so were the words coming out of his mouth.

"Good Morning. I thought you might like some cappuccino from one of Rome's favorite bakeries," he said, passing a cup into my hand.

"Wow, I never expected you, Angelo. How did you find me?" I asked, still standing in the doorway.

"There aren't too many B and B's near the Vatican, and I asked at the front desk of both. Each of the desk clerks know me from touring, and I described you as the beautiful American girl with the puppy. It led me to your door," he answered.

"My, aren't you the clever one," I said with a smile. "I was going to try to find you today anyway. I was wondering if you would like to take me on a day trip to Naples. Perhaps we might stop at a resort or two on our way so I can quiz them about their tennis pro needs?"

"Yes, that would be a very good thing to do. There are several in and around Naples we could check out. Are you thinking you might be staying in Italy permanently?" he quizzed.

"I am thinking I have several loose ends to tie up, and Italy might be in my future," I lied.

"Would you ever consider moving to the States, Angelo?" I hoped his answer would give me a clue as to who he truly was.

"I would love to visit your States, but I, too, have many loose ends here in Italy to move permanently," he said with a sad look.

"Do you have more family in Rome?" I asked.

"No, Miss, I do not. I am hopeful that, one day, I will though," he answered with confidence in his voice. "I am working very hard to tie up my—as you say—loose ends."

"Is there anything I might do to help in your endeavor?" I countered.

"Many are relying on me to handle my business matters very discreetly," he answered, "I would not want to bring you into harm's way."

"It concerns me that you may be in harm's way yourself," I said sincerely. "Perhaps, if it is a legal issue, I can seek help for you from my varied associates."

"I do trust you want to help, but allow me to think further about your offer as we drive toward Naples," Angelo said. "Get ready for our trip, and I will pick you up in about an hour."

As I closed my door, my heart felt as though I were finally getting closer to learning the truth. My concentration was broken as I heard loud voices coming from down the hallway. It sounded like Angelo was involved, and within seconds, I heard a fight break out. I had watched enough television to recognize the sound of someone being overpowered and shoved back and forth against the narrow walls. It sounded like four or five men were beating up Angelo!

Dare I open my door and risk becoming involved? It took only a brief moment for me to sling my door wide open and see the eyes of Angelo's attackers. I shouted at the top of my lungs that I would call the police if they didn't stop. As their eyes met mine and they backed away from Angelo, one man pointed my way and said, "Do not interfere with this matter or harm will come your way. We know who you are." Before they turned around to leave, one man lifted his leg and kicked Angelo directly in the stomach. "Take that!" he said, "Mind what we told you, or we will hurt your American lady friend, too."

CHAPTER 39

B EFORE I COULD REACH down to pull Angelo inside my door, Shiloh flew
out and started chasing after the men. My response was immediate,
and I headed down the hall yelling Shiloh's name a dozen times. His little
body never turned once at the sound of my voice, and because of him, I
was able to see the car and license number as they drove away. I repeated
the information in my head: *Blue Volvo, number AP350; blue Volvo, number
AP350.*

I grabbed the little one and headed back inside to check on Angelo. Blood
was everywhere in the hallway, and one of the thugs had left his handprint
on the floor next to Angelo's head. I reached down to check his pulse and
made sure he was still alive. He was. Thank God. I pulled him by his arms
back into my bungalow apartment. Shiloh followed, and I closed the door.
I immediately grabbed a piece of newspaper and went back into the hall. I
placed the paper over the handprint and got a decent match. Thank you,
CSI, for all the tricks of the trade. I made sure I double bolted my door once
inside again.

Without another thought, I reached for my camera and snapped two
quick pictures of Angelo's face before I attempted to remove the blood that
was starting to harden.

"Angelo, can you hear me? You're safe now. The men have gone. Please,
say something."

"Where am I?" Angelo murmured.

"You are in my apartment. No one can get to you. Where does it hurt?"
I asked.

"I ache all over, but my right eye seems to be clouding over. Am I still
bleeding?" he questioned.

"No, I have stopped the bleeding. Your eye is puffy and starting to close.
Let me grab some ice—I'll be right back."

As I left his side, my mind started reeling with what I would have to do next. This was not a random mugging. They had looked directly at me and told me to stay out of their business. *Did I actually use the word* business *just now? Near-death experience is what I would call it. Oh my gosh, they also told Angelo they would have no problem in hurting his "American lady friend."* My rewinding of the situation was interrupted by Shiloh barking at the door.

My first instinct was not to answer it. So was my second and third instinct. I simply went over to Angelo, put my finger to my lips to hush him, and let Shiloh bark to his heart's content. Whoever it was left after only two knocks. There was silence once again in both the hallway and my bungalow—enough silence to help me remember that I needed to write down the license of that blue Volvo. Please, dear God, help me remember that dang number. Instantly, the plate appeared in my mind: *AP350.*

"I can call the police if you want me to, Angelo," I said. "I know their car and have their plate number. I also have a hand print of one of the men who who was beating you up. You tell me what we should do."

"No! No!" Angelo exclaimed, "We cannot call the police. I will be fine. They did not hurt you, right?"

"They did not hurt me, but they did yell that they knew who I was. They told me I should not interfere with them. Who were those people, Angelo? How do they know us?"

"Please, Miss, let me rest. I will tell you everything soon … very soon," he whispered.

As I watched his eyes close and his body slump, I knew I was in something deeper than I had bargained for originally. I lifted his head and placed a pillow under it. I moved from the doorway and sat at my desk. Just catching my breath took another minute. I looked up to find an e-mail from Michael waiting to be opened on my computer.

"Carrie, no luck yet on post office box address or name on MoneyGrams. Still researching. Are you any closer to verifying A. G. 's validity? Does he trust you yet? How else can I help? I find I am doing more than missing you. Michael."

I placed my hands on my head and bent over my desk. I'll just close my eyes until Angelo wakes up. And then I'll figure out the next piece of the puzzle.

CHAPTER 40

I AWOKE TO ANGELO moaning. It took me a brief second, and then I was on the floor by his side. I noticed blood starting to ooze from his forehead once again, and I wet a cloth to stop the bleeding. I reached into my makeup bag and grabbed the small plastic bottle I had filled just before boarding my flight. I had poured hydrogen peroxide into it knowing that, if I cut myself abroad, I would need it. My mind raced back, for a split second, to growing up and having my mother doctor my knees after falling from my bike. *Perhaps our past truly does dictate our present,* I thought.

As I poured the peroxide over his cuts, I continued telling Angelo all was well. I told him I would find him some pain pills soon. After believing I had warded off any infection, I once again started looking through by bags for any type of medication. My eyes found a bottle of amoxicillin, which I had gotten down in Mexico for an infection, and a prescription bottle full of strong ibuprofen I had picked up for a toothache a few months prior. I made sure Angelo swallowed both pills before I placed his head back on the pillow. His eye was swollen shut, and I placed a plastic bag of ice cubes over it, watching as he fell back asleep.

I knew I did well in a crisis situation, but I felt my body trembling. I reached for a bottle of Riesling and poured myself a glass. I wondered if Angelo had any relatives in Rome. I reached under the bed for my suitcase and pulled out the portfolio Dr. Gabel had given me.

It only took me five minutes before I found my answer: "No known relatives in Rome." Lovely. I contemplated calling the police, but I decided against it. Their questions would be far too numerous and way too detailed for me to even begin answering. At least not until I talked to Angelo—a rational Angelo.

I decided to go out into the hallway and clean up some of the blood accumulation around Angelo's body. I grabbed a sponge and some water and opened my door. As I walked closer to the place where I had lifted up his body, I noticed the floor had already been cleaned. It was spotless. The walls had no blood spattering, and it was as if no confrontation had ever taken place. I quietly walked back into my apartment, closed the door, and leaned up against it. Either management was Johnny-on-the-spot or someone didn't want any evidence hanging around.

I looked toward Angelo. He was still asleep. Shiloh was lying pressed to his side. I knew firsthand that animals could sense sickness. They often stayed as close to an individual as possible for comfort's sake. Shiloh had never left my mother's side after she had fallen, and my mind flooded with memories as I stood looking at the two of them asleep on the floor. It seemed like the perfect time to get inspiration.

"Jesus, Thou are watching over us to bless and care for us. Yes! Remember that always. Out of darkness I am leading you to light. Out of unrest to rest. Out of disorder to order. Out of failure to perfection. Trust me wholly. Fear nothing. Hope ever. Look ever up to Me and I will be your sure aid."

One minute after I closed my book, the phone rang. Of course, my first thought was not to answer it. If *they* knew where I lived, they also knew how to reach me by phone. No one else would be calling me except Dr. Gabel, and it seemed strange that he would try to reach me mid-morning. His last call actually awakened me. By the fourth ring, I had rationalized all possibilities, and by the fifth ring, I knew I would simply ignore it. There was not a sixth ring. Silence once again in my apartment. *Dear Lord, I definitely need your sure aid this very day. Help me to be strong and do as You say and fear nothing.*

I went to the cupboard and pulled out something I knew would settle me down. I had packed it in my luggage because I wasn't sure whether I could find it in Italy. Plus, I wasn't sure how far I would have to walk to a grocery store. I reached for a spoon and plopped down next to Angelo and Shiloh. As I twisted the cap off of my peanut butter and dipped my spoon into the creamy mixture, a smile came over my face. Some tastes just make you forget about the stress of a day.

CHAPTER 41

SEVERAL MORE HOURS DRAGGED by, and I continued doctoring Angelo's forehead. The phone persisted in ringing at thirty-minute intervals, and as time elapsed, it became more clear what my next move would be. As I waited for Angelo to awaken, I pulled out my suitcase and started throwing in enough clothes for a few days. Because those thugs knew where I lived, the thought occurred to me to take anything with me that they might delight in removing from my bungalow. I reached for the portfolio and slipped it into my bag as well.

I walked over to my computer and decided to send an e-mail to Michael with the latest happenings. Before I could compose my thoughts, another e-mail came in from him. *Good for Michael! I exclaimed internally, He actually got a street address for that post office box in Capri.* There was nothing yet on the name, but at least it was a place to start. I rushed off a reply and told him about my latest decision to take a day trip. He wanted me to be safe, and I didn't know of a better way to keep us all safe. Besides, wasn't everyone always saying it was best to get out of town and let the dust settle? It wouldn't take long for me to do so, and I did think it was best to drive Angelo and Shiloh to the port city of Naples.

"Angelo, wake up," I said with urgency, "Did you drive a car when you came to my bungalow this morning?"

"Yes, I did. It's the black Alfa Romeo along the side street. The keys are in my pocket."

"Angelo," I said, "we need to get out of town for a few days. Do you think I could drive your car down to Naples with you resting in the back seat?"

"It is a good idea. Can you bring the car closer to your doorway and help me down the hallway?"

"Of course I can," I answered as I headed toward my door. "Give me your keys and don't move until I return." It only took my hand on the doorknob to remind myself that I needed to change my appearance before heading out into the light of day. I rushed over to my dresser, grabbed my red wig, pulled it on, and headed out the door.

The fresh smell of bleach in the hallway sent chills down my back, and I slowed down my pace. As I casually walked out into the sunlight, my eyes were attempting to focus on anyone who might be keeping watch. Nothing looked suspicious as I rounded the corner and spotted his black car. I walked up to it and unlocked the driver's door. As I sat down, the first thing my eyes noticed was the stick shift. *Thank you, Dad, for teaching me to drive a standard transmission.* I inched the car around the corner and was able to park not far from my doorway. I was thankful Italians drove on the right side like Americans.

I was already starting to become paranoid, and I couldn't stop my eyes from sweeping back and forth. Because I had seen surveillance on television, I knew anyone watching could be as far as a block or two away. With that thought in mind, I restarted the car and decided to drive around for a few minutes to see if anyone would follow. As I rounded the first block, my eyes caught a silver BMW a couple cars back. I don't know why I noticed it—perhaps because it shined unusually brightly in the sunlight. I decided to make a two-block radius and head back to my B and B. By the third turn, I knew I was being followed.

It had only happened to me once before, but I remembered it well. I was driving home in my Datsun Sportster convertible after a movie in Tucson at about 1 a.m. A car with a loud radio blaring approached me on the right side. A single man was staring at me. He kept moving his car closer and closer, and suddenly, he pulled ahead of me and started slowing down. My reaction time was impressive. I made a hard right turn and drove over a curb to pull in front of an all-night convenience store. I ran inside, called the police, and he was gone.

I knew I needed to leave the Vatican area and find more cars and more people. It would be the only way to shake them and provide a space to return to my place to grab Angelo. Timing was everything, and I found myself praying for an obstruction to hinder that silver BMW. My answer came as if on cue. I had just made it through one light when a policeman stepped out into traffic behind me and stopped all the cars—three across and six deep—to allow a funeral procession to drive by. *Thank you, dear God, for this opportunity. I won't waste it.*

I made a right turn and headed back to my bungalow. I really couldn't tell whether there were marked lanes on the roads, but I knew that zigzagging was going to be my fastest way back. It actually was exhilarating to move in and out of traffic as if on a go-kart course. Before I knew it, I was parked outside my bungalow. It only took me two minutes to grab my bag, computer, and Shiloh. I tossed everything in the car. I headed back for Angelo, and he was already standing up, ready for me. He could lean on me, and together, we made it to the car.

I found myself breathing hard until I managed to find the road that led south to Naples. My grip on the steering wheel was gradually loosening. Shiloh had settled down on the passenger seat, and Angelo was resting comfortably in the back seat. I would not feel completely out of the woods until the lights of Naples found my eyes, though.

CHAPTER 42

Angelo had started to get his color back about the time we got to the outskirts of Naples. His swollen eye was opening wider and wider, and only the deep purple hues told the whole story.

"I don't suppose you have any suggestions on where we might stay for a day or two?" I asked.

"Actually, I do. There is a picturesque hotel facing the sea not far from where we are right now. Hotel Bella Capri is only a short walk to the Beverello Pier, and if we are lucky, one of their eight rooms will be available. Please ask at the desk for a room with a view over the entire Gulf of Naples. You will truly enjoy this place if we can get in," Angelo said.

By the time we pulled up in front of Hotel Bella, night had fallen, and the beauty of the city was shining brightly. I decided to leave Angelo and Shiloh in the car. I was able to make a reservation for a few nights with little trouble. Their staff was young and friendly, and within minutes, we were inside one of their clean and spacious rooms. It was such a relief to be able to wind down and not worry about being followed or interrupted.

One of the things I learned from being an apartment dweller in the States was to always grab a bottle of wine as I headed out the door and over to someone else's apartment. Because of this learned routine, I was able to bring a bottle out from my bag and pour a couple glasses for us.

"Such fine wine," Angelo said as he sipped some of my Riesling. "I can hardly believe you remembered to bring a bottle with you."

"Let's just say that I am hopeful I remembered all the right things to bring on our sudden trip south," I said. "I am pleased you like the wine. It seems a perfect end to a hurried day."

As I finished my wine, I started unpacking. I opened one of the two beds so Angelo could get more rest. I was able to help move him from the couch, and he was asleep almost before his head hit the pillow. Shiloh jumped up, cuddled in next to him, and the night was mine.

I knew I needed to draw a warm bath. As I sipped my wine, the happenings of the day circled around in my head. I couldn't help but wonder what another girl—chosen as Dr. Gabel's liaison—would have done under the same circumstances. Would she have had the nerve to open her door and yell at Angelo's attackers? Would she have thought to get a handprint, take pictures, and make sure his bleeding was stopped? And lastly, would she have thought to make sure she wasn't followed as she got out of town? Perhaps not. But then again, perhaps that fictional liaison wouldn't have placed herself in such a dilemma.

I always had good instincts, and someone or something told me we needed to move from that volatile situation. So we ended up in Naples, the Mediterranean port city, the city closest to the post office box of Angelo's MoneyGrams, and the place where I could hopefully uncover Angelo's true identity.

CHAPTER 43

I SLEPT THROUGH THE night and hoped the morning would start off with both of us in good spirits. Angelo was up before I was and in the shower. I saw he had already been out and about. He bought a pair of shorts and a T-shirt, and he was ready for the day ahead of us. He had placed two cappuccinos and croissants on the table, which told me he was physically feeling much better. It was a good time for me to decide our course of action. Somehow I needed to get Angelo to open up with me and share his life. Saving him from serious injuries was a great start. *Please, dear God, help me open the line of communication between us.*

"I can see your eye is looking better. The color is less noticeable," I said as Angelo walked into the living area.

"Yes. I feel 100 percent better today," he said, "How can I thank you for taking me out of harms way?"

"You have already thanked me by recuperating as fast as you have," I said. "I also am thankful for the goodies you brought up to our room. You can tell me why those men were trying to beat you up, however."

"It is a long story. I am not sure I should be involving you," he said, looking down.

"You have already involved me, Angelo. Those men yelled that they knew who I was, and they would have no problem hurting me. How do you know those men?"

"In order for me to tell you who those men are, I would first like to take you to meet someone very special in my world," he said. "It is not very far from here. At the Bella, we are basically in the center of Naples. We will need to drive down the coast for a short while. Would you indulge me this request?"

"Angelo, I want so very much to trust you," I whispered. I stood up, walked over to him, and looked him directly in his eyes. "Do not betray this trust. I will go with you to meet your special someone."

By the time I had walked Shiloh around the Piazza del Municipio and had Angelo tell me the history of the odd, yet beautiful castle that loomed over the harbor, we were ready to head out for the day. I was grateful Angelo felt well enough to drive his car. I was more than willing to ride in the passenger seat holding Shiloh.

It seemed as though we had just started our trip when Angelo pulled into a parking space on the wharf. We were overlooking a huge boat. At least it appeared to be a boat—I soon learned it was something called a hydrofoil, and we would be boarding it to the Isle of Capri. *Thank you, God, for putting Angelo and me on the right path to unfolding this mystery.* I found myself as excited as a child when I learned it would be cruising out at eighty miles per hour, actually hovering over the water.

"Are you certain you aren't just guessing what might please me instead of heading off to meet your special someone?" I asked.

"I assure you, this is the way to meet her," he said with a smile on his face.

As we cruised along, Angelo's profession kicked into gear, and he told me about the Italian island off the Sorrentine Peninsula, which had been a resort since the time of the Roman Republic. We continued to pass ships in the morning fog as we neared Capri. Looking up, I was told, was Vesuvius, an active volcano that buried Pompeii in 79 AD. As we got nearer and nearer, I was shown the many beautiful villas overlooking the sea.

"It is not my intention to make you wait for your upcoming meeting with my special someone, but would you not like for me to show you the beautiful Blue Grotto now that we have arrived at Capri?" he asked.

"I would love to see anything you feel is beautiful, Angelo."

I definitely felt in capable hands as we walked off the amazing hydrofoil, and within minutes, we were in a motorboat. And then we were in a small rowboat just big enough for the two of us and Shiloh. I'm certain the expression and excitement on my face pleased Angelo as we found ourselves outside a small cave. I was told to bend down in the boat as we slipped into a small opening filled with water and darkness. The sunlight passing through the underwater cavity and shining through the seawater created a blue reflection that illuminated the cavern.

It was breathtaking. Angelo explained that the enchantment of the place went back to when the Romans knew of its existence and placed antique statues throughout the grotto.

As we headed back to Capri, I could not help but thank Angelo for the side trip. I could tell he was pleased, and we soon found our way onto a tram heading straight up over the cliffs. Once we arrived at the top, I was amazed to find numerous shops (as well as many inviting places with outside tables). We decided to settle in and enjoy some wine and cheese.

"I have to tell you, Angelo, I am very impressed with *your* Italy," I said smiling.

"It is not just *my* Italy," he said with a wink. "I continue to be impressed every day with Italy, and I promise you that our trip away from Rome is far from over."

CHAPTER 44

AFTER HAVING A PLEASANT tasting merlot, I eased back in my chair and let the sunlight warm my face. I thought, *Angelo looks so youthful. How could someone so young have so many secrets?* I debated how much I would share with him. I, too, had secrets. Perhaps it was time for both of us to lay our cards on the table. It needed to be Angelo first, of course.

"I am more than ready to meet your someone special, Angelo," I said.

"Then I am more than ready to introduce you," he answered. "It is not far from here. We can walk and window shop as we go."

The shops were numerous, and all sold beautiful, indescribable works of art. I was mesmerized as we walked the narrow paths checking out colorful pottery, oil paintings, fresh-made sugar cones, jewelry, perfumes made on the island from local herbs, made-to-order sandals, lemon liquor, and on and on.

I could not help but notice the name of the main pathway with all the quaint shops was the same as the one on the Western Union MoneyGrams. My heart jumped as I thought I might be able to find the exact address that Michael had e-mailed me. I reached into my purse and found the numbers. My eyes started searching each store front for the matching three digits. There didn't seem to be any rhyme or reason—and certainly no continuity in the three numbers over each doorway.

After about forty-five minutes, we were walking down a narrow pathway that led to a stone church. It was set off from the storefronts, and it seemed almost out of place. An undersized fence surrounded a playground in the back, and even though it was hard to see, it looked as if children were playing some form of kickball. A huge bell tower was off to our left, and as we approached, I glanced up and noticed the year 1489 set in stone at the top. We continued walking toward two huge doors, and my eyes caught numbers burned into one of them. As we neared the door, I squinted and barely made out the numbers. *Oh my gosh, the numbers were identical to the numbers on*

Angelo's MoneyGrams! Was it possible he was sending the money here each week? Perhaps I had judged him too harshly. Dear lord, please help me have an open mind throughout this day.

"This is the church I attended as a boy," Angelo said, looking around.

We continued walking down several hallways, and soon we came to a closed door. As Angelo opened it, we found ourselves staring at several robes and vestments. I was surprised when Angelo parted the hangers and walked another several feet, deeper into the closet. As I watched in awe, he bent down and pulled up a trapdoor on the floorboards.

"Do not be afraid," he said, "Go before me and take the stairway down. I will close the doors and follow close behind you."

It was as if I were in a Nancy Drew mystery novel and had just discovered a hidden chamber. For whatever reason, I did as Angelo directed and headed down the stairs.

"This way," he said as he grabbed my hand. We continued walking through a stone-built tunnel.

The smell was musty and damp, and I said a quick prayer in the hopes that we would not be in the cramped passageway very long. I found myself having to duck down lower and lower as we continued on. With every step, I felt Shiloh's body getting more tense. After endless turns, we found ourselves in front of yet another door. Angelo gave two quick knocks and then another three. Silence. My curiosity was really piqued by this time. After several seconds, the door opened.

"Angelo, please come in," she said with a wavering voice, "I was not aware you were coming for a visit, or I would have greeted you out front with the children."

"Do not worry about it, sister," Angelo said. "I have brought someone to meet you. She has become a good friend of mine. She even saved my life recently."

Before I could digest what was being said, my hand was being held by a sweet-looking, older nun who wore a dear smile and a frayed black and white habit.

"My name is Sister Mary B., and any friend of Angelo's is welcome here. I hope you and your *cucciolo* have not had too long a journey. I am assuming you are here to meet Angelo's brothers and sister?"

"Ah, Sister, I am not sure why I am here," I said, looking back at Angelo.

Angelo was smiling as he walked over to hug both of us. After the three of us hugged, I felt more at peace than I had felt since I landed in Italy.

"I have a great deal to explain, Sister, but I'm certain you can allow me several minutes in one of the classrooms, no?" Angelo begged.

"Of course, Angelo. Please take your time. And when you come out, we will announce your presence to the children," she said.

CHAPTER 45

ANGELO GRABBED MY HAND, and we walked down a hallway with school rooms on both sides. It certainly surprised me to find all of that space underneath a church. My curiosity was piqued thinking about the statement Sister Mary B. had made about his brothers and sister. We eventually found our way into a library and sat down facing one another.

"I feel I owe you an explanation of my life after all you have done for me," Angelo started. "I never knew my parents very well. Nor did my brothers or sister. My father left our home soon after my youngest brother was born. When I was five, my mother took all of us over to my uncle's home in Rome for a visit. She left on the premise of seeking work, and she never returned. My aunt and uncle were raising their own children, and they could not manage to feed four more mouths.

"That is when we were all brought to this mission and asked to be raised by the nuns. There are no orphanages in this area, and these underground rooms were tunneled many centuries ago by monks who sought to house and feed the needy children. Over the years, many nuns have rescued hundreds who have been dropped at their door without any questions asked. They have provided education, nurturing, and love for those of us who had no one else. The small community surrounding this mission closes their eyes to the needs of the abandoned children. As far as the people of Capri are concerned, this safe house does not exist."

As I sat there, listening to Angelo, my mind thought back to all the insignificant worries I had growing up. "What dessert would I have after our dinner meal? How many presents would I have on my birthday? What new dress would I wear to school?" *Dear Lord, I am so sorry for taking so much for granted.*

"Go on," I said.

"As we grew," he said, "we were given the love and appreciation for caring and sharing with one another. When I got old enough, I moved out and went to live with my uncle in Rome. My aunt had passed away, and he welcomed the company. He owns a religious shop across from the Vatican, and I am able to sleep in a small room in the back of his store. He was the one who helped me become a tour guide."

I was soon putting things together in my mind. *His uncle must be the older gentleman I met on the airplane. It must be the same shop I was in when I overheard the voices discussing sending money every Wednesday.*

"What is the name of your uncle's shop?" I asked. "I have been in a small religious store across from the Vatican."

"The name is *Angelo di Luce,* he said. It means *Angel of Light.*"

My eyes widened, and I thought back to how I had always been told there were no coincidences.

"Go on," I said again.

"As soon as I found a job, I began sending money every week back to Sister Mary Bryant. My uncle introduced me to several other young men who had been raised by the nuns (and who also have siblings still here). We all got together, and I was designated to collect money from all and send it directly to Capri."

I smiled and looked directly into Angelo's eyes. "You are a good man, and I am so very proud to know you. Is there more?"

"Yes, unfortunately, there is more," he said. "One day, about six months ago, I was buying a MoneyGram, and two men followed me out to my car. They told me they knew I was sending money to feed and hide many abandoned children. They said that if I wanted the children and nuns to be safe—and not have the province of Naples take action against us—I would need to double the amount sent each week.

"I met with the others. Most of us agreed: we needed to protect the children and the nuns. By all of us taking a second job, we were able to provide additional monies. These people had men everywhere, and they insisted that I start sending to a post office box in place of a physical address at the mission. By doing this, they could intercept the money and take their share before handing over the difference to the nuns. These men became more greedy over time, and they wanted a higher and higher percentage.

"The men in my group became conflicted over what to do and how much to send. At our last meeting at my uncle's shop, several wanted to stop sending any money and risk the well-being of the children. They persuaded me not to double the money one week and see what happened."

"Oh my gosh!" I exclaimed, "That's why those thugs beat you up!"

"Yes, and that is where you came to my rescue," he said with appreciation.

CHAPTER 46

THE NOISE OUT IN the hallway was loud enough to make both of our heads turn and look at the closed door. At first, I thought children were running in from the playground and finding their classrooms. Because the noise did not subside—and we both heard several nuns raising their voices—it didn't take Angelo long to open our door and question what was happening.

"Sister," he begged, "what is all the commotion?"

"I am so sorry to tell you, Angelo, but your youngest brother has been taken by a stranger from the playground. Please, please, help us go outside and look for him."

"But Sister, how do you know this? Which of the children actually saw it happen?" Angelo questioned.

"It was Pedro, and he held onto your brother's leg, trying to stop him from being pulled over the fence. Here is Stephano's shoe."

"Oh my God, Sister, you are right!" Angelo exclaimed. He reached for my hand, and immediately we were all running down a hallway, up a staircase, and into the enclosed yard in the back. Our eyes were scanning back and forth, and we all separated (taking different paths across the grounds). Angelo found his way to the highest part of the yard, and he leaped the fence in one easy maneuver. Before I blinked, he was running along the side of the church toward the front entrance. As I caught my breath, I noticed five elderly nuns outside in the yard, gathering all the other children and rushing them inside.

My immediate thought was to locate Angelo and help with the search in front of the mission. *Please, dear Lord, help us find this frightened child.* I ran over to the same area of the yard where I saw Angelo scale the fence, and I did a scissor kick to reach the other side. Poor Shiloh had no idea what was going on, and he stayed pressed against my side. As I ran along, I found myself yell Stephano's name over and over until I spotted Angelo.

"Have you seen him yet?" I called.

"No, I have seen nothing!" he answered, "I don't have a good feeling about this. Why was it only *my* brother this man decided to take? I am thinking this has something to do with those men who beat me up back in Rome."

"I was thinking the very same thing," I said with resolve. "Do we need to contact the authorities?"

"No, we cannot," Angelo answered, "By so doing, it would only bring attention to the children who are here. Come, let us take my car and head back into town. Maybe we will get lucky and catch a glimpse of Stephano." He reached into his billfold, pulled out a picture, and handed it to me. I could instantly see the resemblance.

Angelo had the car started and in gear before my door was even closed. I was frantically surveying the wooded area on both sides as we neared Capri's main street. We both agreed to park, separate, and check in each shop for any sign of his younger brother (or of a man forcing a child to accompany him).

The two of us decided to take opposite sides of the cobblestone street and check inside each individual shop. We agreed to notify each other with a head shake if anyone suspicious was found. After we had both gone in and out of many shops—for about thirty minutes—a wild fear was starting to form in my mind: *What on earth will we do if he is nowhere to be found?*

I continued my search for another half hour before Angelo met me outside of a pottery shop. I could tell by the look in his eyes and the expression on his face how defeated he felt. I wasn't sure what he would tell me, but I knew it would be a well-thought-out plan.

"Okay, nothing," he said. "We need to head back to the mission to verify no other children have been taken. If, in fact, Stephano was their target, we will hear from whoever took him. They definitely want more than my brother. They are money hungry vultures, and they will use any means to meet their needs. They are, most likely, very angry we were able to dodge them and get out of Rome so quickly. Come, let us find the car and be on our way."

CHAPTER 47

A s we pulled up to the mission, I followed Angelo around the back and up some stairs to another wooden door. He pulled out a key, and we found ourselves inside a small alcove. Yet another key opened a similar doorway, which led us into the sacristy behind the altar. I looked around to see altar linens, sacred vessels, and vestments along one side. The back wall had numerous crucifixes and crosses leaning against it, and the smell of incense was ever so faint. I watched as Angelo bent down on one knee and pulled a discolored mat away from a section on the floor. My eyes caught a small brass ring, and within seconds, he was pulling on it to expose a trapdoor.

"Please, head down the stairway. I will be right behind you," Angelo said.

We were once again heading downward, below the main church. We found ourselves in the back of a small classroom. I waited for Angelo's lead, and he grabbed my hand as we headed out into a hallway and ran right into Sister Mary B.

"Sister, we have searched many Capri shops, and we have not found Stephano," he said exasperated. "Did you do a count of the children. Were any others taken?"

"No other children are missing," she said, "but one of Stephano's best friends found this envelope on the playground with your name on it." Sister Mary B. handed it to Angelo, and I watched as his face became sullen.

He tore open the envelope and began reading out loud: "We are finished playing games. American to bring $50,000 in exchange for boy. No *polizia*. You have seventy-two hours."

My heart stopped beating for a brief second. Not only did they have Angelo's brother, but they also mentioned me and a great deal of money. Those facts alone were mind-boggling, but the one fact that stood out was that we couldn't involve the police.

"What are we going to do?" I questioned, looking around.

"I am not sure," Angelo said.

"We are going to all sit down and figure this situation out," Sister Mary B. added. "But before we do that, we are going to say a silent prayer for poor Stephano."

As we bowed our heads and closed our eyes, I heard myself saying my prayer out loud: "Please, dear Lord, protect Angelo's brother. Keep him safe from any harm or danger. And, dear Jesus, help us come up with a plan to bring him home safely."

"Thank you so much for your prayer," Angelo said. "Sister, I think I should talk to the children to calm their fears before supper hour."

"I agree, Angelo," Sister Mary B. said, "I'll gather them in the library. You can meet me there in a few minutes."

It finally occurred to me how much time had elapsed since I had been in touch with Michael or Dr. Gabel. *Perhaps one of the nuns has a computer so I can send off a quick e-mail while Angelo is meeting with the children,* I thought. *I certainly don't want to worry anyone in my life, and no one really knows I am on the Isle of Capri.*

"Sister," I asked, "would it be possible to use one of the school's computers for a short while?"

"Why, of course. There is one in my office. Please take this hallway to the end. My office is on the right."

As I walked down the gloomy hallway (devoid of any sunlight), all I could think about were the lives of the dedicated spiritual leaders and the good they were doing each and every day. What a shame they all had to be hidden away from mainstream life. It didn't take me long to log into my e-mail account and see that I had six different messages from Michael. I quickly read them and sent off my own: "Michael: I am so sorry for not responding sooner. Much has happened this past week. I have confirmed Angelo is one of the good guys. But the bad guys have been literally after us. We are now in Capri, south of Rome (at the address confirmed by you on the MoneyGrams). It is a mission church, and many children are being housed by local nuns underneath the structure. Angelo's brother has been taken, and he is in grave danger without monies from us. You mentioned Dr. Gabel calling you. How did that transpire? E-mail me when you receive this. Carrie."

I had no sooner sent off my e-mail when a reply came in. It was from Michael, and I could tell he was upset just by the tone of the e-mail: "Carrie: Finally I hear from you! Thank God you are safe. I am sitting in your B and B in Rome. I lied and told them I was your brother from the States, and they let me right in. (So much for tight security in Italy.) I have been here for two days now. I have rented a car, and I will be heading your way. Do not attempt to save the world without my help! Dr. Gabel tried calling you here in Rome, and when you didn't answer, he requested your in-case-of-emergency-name from the desk clerk. Evidently, you put down my name and number ... I feel flattered. After the two of us talked over the phone, he thought it wise for me to fly over to make sure all was okay on your end. I am officially on his payroll now and coming to your rescue. (Just trying to bring a smile to your face, neighbor.) Missy will be taken care of by Mandie. You will be taken care of by *me*. See you soon! Michael."

Wow! Quite an e-mail, I thought. Just hearing from Michael brought me some sense of comfort. Never in my wildest imagination would I have thought he would fly all the way to Italy to make sure I was safe. Perhaps I had not given him all the credit he deserved. My thoughts about Michael were soon interrupted by Angelo, however.

"Were you able to get through to your friend in the States?" he asked.

"Yes," I answered. "Were you able to settle down the children?"

"I had a long talk with all of them. I would like to introduce you to all the children as well as my brother and sister who are still here," he said.

"Before we do that, Angelo," I said, "there is more we need to talk about. Much more."

CHAPTER 48

I HAD NO IDEA how I was going to explain to Angelo who I really was and my true purpose for being in Italy. Dr. Gabel wanted me to be extremely careful with his identity and his benefactor status. I was, however, under no direct order to hide my job description from Angelo once I verified he was who he claimed to be: a young man trying to help his siblings and other children in a rundown, nun-staffed sanctuary under a church. *Dear Lord, please guide my actions and my lips to help Angelo understand my mission is just.*

"Angelo," I started, "I have so very much to tell you. I want you to first believe I am doing everything in my power to bring your brother home safely. A good friend of mine will be arriving soon in order to help us expedite a plan. Before he arrives, I must tell you who I truly am and why I am here in Italy."

"What do you mean *who you are?*" Angelo asked.

"Please sit down and listen to me. I was hired by someone who would like to—"

"Angelo, please come out quickly! Your brother has returned!" Sister's Mary B.'s voice was high-pitched and loud … extremely loud.

We both reacted instantly and flew out of the small classroom and into a narrow hallway. Standing before us was a small boy who had matted dark black hair and smudges on his face and arms. He was wearing only one shoe. His breathing sounded as if he had run for blocks without stopping, and dried tears marked his face.

"Stephano, how did you get here?!" Angelo shouted as he raced to hug his brother.

"I waited until those mean men went to sleep, and then I sneaked out a small window, putting me on a roof." Stephano was talking very fast, and his throat sounded raspy and in need of water. "I remembered how you taught me to shimmy down trees, so I found a rain gutter and slid down it. I ran all the way here because I knew you would be worried about me."

Within a short period of time, Sister Mary B. had brought Stephano a glass of water, Angelo had his brother sitting down on a chair, and I had found a damp cloth to wipe away the smudges from his face and arms. The closer I found myself to him, the more my senses picked up on the smell of vanilla and cinnamon. *What on earth?* I wondered. All at once, it came to me: candles. They must have had him in a candle-making shop.

"Stephano," I questioned, "did you happen to notice what kind of place they were hiding you in? Did it smell like candles?"

"Yes, Miss, it smelled just like candles," he answered. "I did not see the place, though, because they tied a blindfold over my eyes and something around my hands. They took me up some stairs and forced me to sit in a chair. When they were snoring, I worked at getting free. I saw light from a window. I climbed on some boxes and was able to get away."

"We are so very proud of you," Sister Mary B. said. "Please come into the kitchen. I will find you some food."

CHAPTER 49

As I checked my watch, it occurred to me that Michael would be arriving at the mission any minute. I left the small group eating in the kitchen with Sister Mary B., and I made my way to the front of the church. It was, by no means, an easy task. I had only entered through the front doors once, and I had been ushered by Angelo into a closet to head down into the basement area. Retracing my steps was out of the question, so I headed out into the backyard where Stephano had originally been kidnapped. Shiloh was more than happy to exercise his little legs, and in no time, we were standing in front, waiting for Michael to show up.

The moonlight was playing tricks with my eyes, and I kept thinking I saw the image of a person coming our way. I hadn't felt Shiloh's body start to shake and his tail start to wag since I left the States. It was as if he knew it was Michael walking up the path. My inner excitement was contagious. As the silhouette made it to the bell tower, I started walking over to greet him. I saw that fantastic smile. Within seconds, he was hugging the two of us. His cologne reminded me instantly how much I had missed him, and I returned the hug.

"Thank you so much for coming all this way," I said sheepishly.

"Are you kidding? I'd go anywhere for you and this little guy," he said, petting Shiloh's head.

"Let me look at you," he remarked as he smiled and pushed me back to within arms' length.

"Please don't look too hard at me, it's been a very long day," I said and smiled back. "You hold Shiloh and follow me around to the back of this church. We should really get inside and out of the darkness. I don't trust the night around here yet."

As I turned to lead the way, Michael put a hand on my shoulder and came up next to me. He took my face with his hand and moved my head ever so gently to meet his lips. The kiss happened so suddenly that I found myself totally engulfed in the spontaneous act. As his arms reached around me, the thought of our first kiss filtered back into my mind. I thought, *This kiss is definitely more passionate.* I did not want it to end.

"I have missed you so very much, Carrie," he said. "I would have never forgiven myself if something had happened to you while I was back in the States. I should have made time and come with you. Are you sure you are all right?"

"I'm fine, but I already feel better with you here," I said. His arms did not release me.

"So much has happened since I've seen you last," I said with a sigh. "It's really great Dr. Gabel is paying you to fly all this way. I'm hoping the two of us can figure out a solution for Angelo, his siblings, and all the other children living under this church. It's really a sad, sad situation."

"I'm certain we can come up with a plan," Michael said, slowly releasing me from his arms. "Let's head inside."

As we headed toward the back of the church and over the fence, Michael watched in disbelief as I guided him in and out of the dark shadows to an old, wooden door. Of course, I didn't know whether I could get anyone's attention to let us in, and I even surprised myself by knocking the same knock Angelo had used earlier. It didn't take very long before it opened and we were face to face with Sister Mary B.

"Please come in," she said, "Angelo told me you were expecting a friend, so I was just finishing up in the kitchen while waiting for you to find your way back in. Are you two hungry?"

"No, Sister," I said, "This is my good friend, Michael, from the States, and between the two of us, we intend to make your life easier."

That would be wonderful, but God provides and watches over all of us," she said. "I certainly do not want you two in the middle of all this mess."

Michael looked directly at her and said, "Sister, no one should have to live in fear, especially children and their caregivers. Now if you will kindly show us where we might find a couple rooms to get a good night's sleep, we can discuss more of this in the morning."

As she led the way, I found myself finally starting to unwind. Perhaps Michael was right. A good night's rest was just what we needed.

CHAPTER 50

S HILOH WOKE ME EARLY, and I heard the sound of children running up and down the outside hallway. It felt good to remain in bed and to go over all that had happened. I definitely needed to contact Dr. Gabel sometime and get his input on the past few weeks. I couldn't help but think he had connections in Italy who would help us deal with the thugs. Michael and I needed to get as many names as possible before I could verify the recent happenings. I found my heart starting to race just thinking about the magnitude of the work that needed to be accomplished. I reached over to the small table next to my bed and grabbed my devotional. "You need me. I need you. My broken world needs you. Many a weary troubled heart needs you. Many a troubled heart will be gladdened by you. Health—Peace—Joy—Patience—Endurance. They all come from contact with Me. You cannot make too many demands upon Me. Claim what you will."

Perfect, I thought, *I need your help, dear Lord. Guide and direct us so we can find these horrible men. Show us the pathway to bring them to justice. Help us protect these children and their spiritual leaders. Let us feel your guidance.*

I was soon dressed and headed toward Michael's room. As I approached, I noticed his door was open and his room was empty. Hopefully he found his way to the kitchen area. Shiloh's nose was twitching, and it proved accurate: breakfast was already on the table as we entered the room.

"Good morning!" I exclaimed. Michael, Angelo, and Sister Mary B. were already seated at the table.

"Hey, sleepy head!" Michael said, "We were just going to start eating. Angelo and I have introduced ourselves to each other, and we are ready to do some brainstorming after we enjoy some of Sister Mary B.'s cooking."

By the time we all had more than enough food (and Sister had left the room to teach in a classroom), the three of us started discussing our next course of action. Angelo felt he should stay at the mission to safeguard the children and nuns. Michael felt we should be proactive and go back to the post office box location and start from scratch. I felt we needed to pursue the secret location where Stephano was hidden away for any clues.

"Sounds as though we have all come up with a terrific plan for the day," I said. "Angelo, you stay put and keep your eyes open for any intruders. Michael and I will head into Capri and try to come up with why your brother was smelling like candle wax when he ran away yesterday."

"You actually think you smelled candle wax on him?" Angelo asked.

"No, I *know* I smelled it on him," I said with certainty. "My thinking is: we find a shop making candles, we find the men who kidnapped your brother."

"I hope it will be that easy," Angelo said, "Be safe."

I knew Michael's face would not be recognizable to the men we were going to search out. They knew me, however. Therefore, before we headed out, I grabbed my black wig and left Shiloh in my room. As we found our way out the back door, Michael grabbed my hand. It made me feel secure and confident. We were over the low fence in no time. We walked past the church and up the narrow path into town. I took a deep breath knowing our mission was to expose the men who seemed obsessed with acquiring more money than most people made in a lifetime.

CHAPTER 51

I WATCHED MICHAEL'S EYES once we filtered into the stream of tourists mingling in and around all the quaint shops on the main street in Capri. You could see he was on a mission. He was concentrating on storefront names, and I had to remind him we were not just looking for a candle shop—I was also trying to spot any of the thugs I met in the hallway back in Rome.

"Can you describe any of these guys to me so I can help you look?" he asked.

"All three of the men beating up on Angelo had facial hair. I'm not sure what you call it. Actually, I think it's called a *goatee*. Yes, they all had goatees," I said with certainty.

"Anything else about them? Were they muscled up?" he asked.

"No, all three were of thin stature and wearing black T-shirts. But now that you mention it, I did notice a small tattoo on the wrist of the man beating on Angelo when I opened my door. Let me think about it for a while, and I'll try to come up with what I saw."

We continued walking past shop after shop, our eyes constantly moving in every direction. Michael's eyes were looking upward for shop names and into all the window displays for candles. My eyes were searching each and every passerby (as well as shop owners) with the hope of catchiong a glimpse of the Italian men I interrupted outside my B and B.

"You know the chance of us finding these men is slim, right?" I questioned.

"Be patient. We have just started to look and—oh my God! This shop in front of us right now sells candles!" Michael exclaimed.

He was right. Candles of all sizes were on linen doilies on a large table directly in front of the window for all to view. I felt my hand tense inside of Michael's. I certainly didn't believe we would find the shop so soon into our search.

"Just relax, Carrie," he said, "No one knows us, and this probably isn't the only candle shop. Remember, we are tourists. Just go on my lead once we get inside."

The front door was wide open to allow the sunshine and mild breeze of the day to filter into the small shop. The minute we stepped inside, my nose started smelling the multiple scents of vanilla, cinnamon, bayberry, ginger, and apple. Yes, these were the same smells all over Stephano's clothes. I couldn't help but wonder whether they had an upstairs room above their shop. I decided to let Michael start the discussion with whomever approached us.

"Hello, do you speak English?" a young woman with an Italian accent asked.

"Yes, we do," Michael answered. "We are looking for quite a few of your vanilla candles. Don't you think we need about ten dozen, honey?" he asked, looking directly at me.

"Ah, yes, about that many," I answered. "In any case, we need a great deal of them. Perhaps you have more than what we are seeing on your tables? Do you have additional storage space for more candles upstairs?"

"No, Miss, I am so sorry, but we do not have any storage space other than what you are seeing right now. We do not have an upstairs over our shop. There is another candle shop at the end of this plaza, though. I know they have more than enough room for storing additional candles. I am so very sorry I could not help you."

"Thank you anyway," Michael said, "We will check out the other shop. Are there only two candle shops in Capri?" he questioned.

"Yes, sir—only two," she replied with a smile.

I followed Michael out into the sunshine, and we both stared into each other's eyes with a look of hope. Perhaps we were close to helping Angelo. Perhaps we were being guided by a higher power ... the power I had requested hope from earlier in the day.

Tables were set up in the middle of the piazza, and we decided to figure out our next course of action over some wine. We needed to set a plan in motion that would determine the future of Angelo and the children in the mission.

CHAPTER 52

I<small>T WAS REALLY HARD</small> to look into each of the many shop windows and not think about taking home a souvenir. We found that, if we slowly walked down the center of the piazza, it was easy to view the store fronts and their windows. All were narrow, but not all of them were tall enough to support an upstairs room. Stephano was certain he walked up stairs when he was kidnapped and blindfolded, so we had to search accordingly.

I thought back to how confident and strong I was when interviewing for the position of liaison with Dr. Gabel. That independence seemed to be slowly creeping away the more involved I became with Stephano's abductors. Before I could get too deep into thought, Michael placed my hand in his and squeezed it tightly. It made me remember the saying, "There is strength in numbers." *Please, dear God, let the two of us—with Your help—have the strength to carry out our plan.*

"What did that lady say was the name of the shop?" I questioned.

"She said it was *Candela nel Buio,* which I think means *Candle in the Dark,*" he answered.

"And you really think we can pull this off, right?" I asked with some hesitation in my voice.

"Yes, I do. We need to take our tourist act one step further and wait for an opportunity to hide away in the room over their store. Stop worrying. We'll make it happen."

His reassurance was all I needed, and it wasn't long before my eyes caught a glimpse of a cement angel with something in her hand. It looked like a candle, but we needed to venture closer to make sure. I nodded toward the small shop. Michael took my cue, and we headed over to look directly into the window. Sure enough, candles graced not only the angel in the doorway, but also every shelf and table inside. The pleasing, aromatic fragrance of apple and cinnamon grabbed my attention, and my mind raced back in time to being seven and walking into Gram Lamm's kitchen. She always seemed to be baking, and I loved apple pie ever since trying hers.

We ventured into the shop and started picking up candles and smelling them. It seemed as though we had the place all to ourselves. As we walked around table after table, my eyes picked up on what I had hoped we would find: a stairway. I nudged Michael and motioned with my head toward the staircase. There were about ten steps that ended at a closed wooden door.

"No one is around," I whispered, "so I'm heading up those stairs to check out whether the door is open. It doesn't say *not* to go upstairs, so if I'm caught, we can just say I thought more of their candles were on the second level."

I ascended the stairs quickly and quietly. I expected to find the door locked, and I was really surprised to have the knob turn in my hand and open with a screeching noise. My instincts told me to enter and close the door behind me. I knew Michael could fend for himself and cover my tracks if necessary.

It took my eyes a few seconds to adjust to the darkness. Once they did, the first thing I noticed was one chair in the middle of the small, cramped attic. Normally, I would not have given it a second thought, but after hearing Stephano tell the story of how he was tied to a chair, I headed over to it. The chair seemed out of place, but that fact alone would not connect it to the chair Angelo's brother was tied to. I tried to imagine being the kidnapping victim, and I wondered what I would do with tied hands. I sat down in the chair, and then it occurred to me. His abductors would have tied his hands *behind* the chair. I looked over my shoulder to the floor, and there it was: one red shoelace. Stephano's shoelace.

CHAPTER 53

THE COMMOTION BELOW ME got my attention, and after I reached down to pick up the shoelace, I headed to the closed door. I could hear Michael's voice and other male voices. They were saying something about closing the shop and clearing out everyone inside. I glanced down at my watch and hit the button on the side. The dim glow showed me it was only 3:00 p.m. It seemed a little early to close. Michael sounded like he was making that same point. The male voices kept saying *lasciare* over and over, and I knew that meant everyone had to leave.

Once my initial fear of being left hiding in the attic disappeared, I was able to reason out how fortunate I was to (potentially) overhear Stephano's abductors discuss their new plan. I knew Michael would not simply go away; I knew he would be outside in the piazza until I could find my way back to him. *Thank you, God, for this chance. Please continue to protect me.*

It wasn't long before I heard the front door close and the sound of tourist voices subside. I kept trying to make out how many male voices were still in the shop below me. It sounded like three. I got that confirmation when I started to hear footsteps on the stairs—the same stairs that led to the attic and me. Since my eyes had already adjusted to the darkness, I knew the only possible place I could go to avoid being seen. I headed to the darkest corner of the room.

As the attic door creaked open, I saw three men enter. I knew I would either be seen or not, and my prayer was immediate: *Please, God, help me to blend into the darkness.* The only light came from an upper, narrow window, which I assumed was how Stephano got away. It allowed me enough light to barely see their faces. All three men had dark hair. All three men had goatees.

"Listen up," one man whispered, "the boy got away, but we should not let this stop us."

"You know we cannot get into the mission," a second man said, "We have tried time and time again."

The first man shook his head and said, "They do not know this. Emilio has already put pressure on the others in Rome who have brothers and sisters here. They have assured him they will be sending more money to the post office box on Wednesday. We will get this money and decide how we can continue to live—what is it the Americans say?—high on the hog. I have no problem with hurting anyone to make our point. I want to be rich, and I will do anything for American money."

The third man held his hand in the air, and the others followed. They pumped their hands in the air and said in unison, "Forcelli's rule."

It wasn't so much what they said together that got my attention—it was what the dim light exposed on their wrists. All three of them had tattoos of a small Italian flag surrounded by fire. The same tattoo I had seen on the man beating up Angelo back in Rome.

As they turned to walk out of the attic, my foot must have moved. It was just enough to make a small, insignificant sound. The last man turned and looked directly at the corner of the room where I was standing. *Please help me to remain invisible to his eyes.*

"Wait a minute," he said to the others, "I thought I heard something."

"Give it a rest, Tony. You probably heard the mouse we've been trying to catch for a decade now."

As if on cue, he turned back and followed them out the door. I heard their footsteps go down the stairs and out the front door of the shop. Silence, beautiful silence.

CHAPTER 54

S O MUCH TO REMEMBER. Fortunately, I had time to write it all down because there was no way in heck I was heading out the front door until dark. Unless, of course, Michael magically appeared and guided me to safety. Because the chances of that were nil, I sat down, took out a pen and piece of paper from my travel vest (Mandie had given it to me for my trip), and I started making notes.

I attempted to remember every fact—even the smallest—from the time I first met Angelo. I just knew Dr. Gabel would have some influence over the local authorities, and I wanted to be as accurate as possible to put the thugs away for good. By the time I made notations on the front and back page of my piece of paper, I felt the wine from before starting to take effect. *What the heck!* I thought, *I'll just find a small area in the corner behind the boxes and settle in until the night can provide cover for me as I leave the shop.*

What seemed like five minutes turned out to be several hours, and I awoke to something that sounded like a squirrel climbing my screen to get to the bird feeder (back in the United States). I kept still, and I kept hearing the sound. *Please don't let this noise be a rat or something even bigger.* After a short while, I got my courage up and started to meander around. The sound was definitely coming from that high window. *Should I be curious enough to climb a few boxes and check it out?*

Having nothing else to do, I got up on one box and then a second. Finally, I clambered on top of a third box to reach the window. I kept telling myself, *If a ten-year-old boy can do it, so can I.* As I reached the window ledge, the annoying noise got louder. *If I see a rat,* I thought, *I'm literally going to scream.*

As I placed my hands on the ledge and pulled myself up, I found I could look down onto the center of the piazza. Each time I leaned closer to the window, something like fine sand or pebbles would hit the glass. *What on earth? If I can just look down closer to the shop, perhaps I can see what is causing it.* I timed it perfectly, let the scratching subside, and looked directly down. What I saw was unbelievable. It also made me think I was cast as a damsel, about to be rescued in some romantic movie.

It was Michael. I watched him reach down to pick up pebbles and throw them up to my window to get my attention. *Oh my goodness! How long had he been attempting to wake me up?* I pushed open the window and waved my hand. I pulled myself up further to let him see my face.

"Michael, how sweet of you to get my attention! I apologize for not waking up sooner."

"Carrie, thank God you are all right! Can you walk downstairs now and let yourself out the front door?" he asked, "The piazza is very quiet."

"Perfect. I'm on my way."

I had to be really careful in the dark as I hurried down the stairway. For a small shop, they had a lot of tables set up displaying their candles. There didn't seem to be much rhyme or reason to how they had laid them out. I thought my eyes had adjusted to the darkness, but as I turned one way, I ran right into a smaller round table and candles went flying. In an effort to catch the table, I turned my ankle and went down to the floor. I prayed they didn't have a security camera because I'd look like something out of a Peter Sellers' movie.

As I got up and finally found my way to the front door, I hoped all I had to do was turn the knob. As my hand touched the knob, I found it didn't rotate. *Good God, how different can a door knob be from mine in the States?* I fumbled around the knob until I found a small button and pushed it in. Voilà! The door opened, and I made my way out.

CHAPTER 55

Even in the dark, I could see Michael's smile. He grabbed my hand, and we took off running down a back alley on the way to the mission. I'd been in Capri several days longer than Michael, and I had no idea about the shortcut we were taking. Once we got out of sight, we stopped running and found our way beneath a huge tree. As we caught our breath, I noticed Michael staring at me.

"What?" I quizzed.

"I was just looking at the gutsiest woman I've ever known," he said. "You just spent ten hours holed up in the kidnappers' attic, and you don't show any signs of anxiety." He bent forward and kissed me on the forehead.

"Hey, it's only because I knew you were on the outside watching over me," I replied and smiled. "Wait until I tell you what I overheard!"

"Before you tell me, I've got something to tell you," Michael said. "Of course, you knew all of us in the shop were escorted out for the day. I got to thinking about the description you gave me of the one man beating up Angelo, and I noticed all the guys had goatees. You'll never guess what I did."

"Can't imagine. What?"

"I stood across from the shop and waited for the men to leave. And then I got a great picture of them on my phone. I figured, if they were the bad guys, we'd need to prove it."

"Perfect!" I exclaimed, "They *are* the bad guys! I've made notes on everything, and I know exactly what their next move is. I've also got the shoelace used to tie up Stephano."

"Sounds like we make a great team," Michael said. "What do you think about bringing Dr. Gabel into our latest findings?"

"You reading my mind?" I asked as I smiled. "I'm hoping you have a way we can contact the good doctor and fax over all our findings."

"I have a number, and I think we can find a fax machine somewhere on the Isle of Capri. Tell me we aren't involved in their next maneuver," he asked.

"Not if Dr. Gabel has local law enforcement contacts."

The two of us were still pumped up on adrenaline by the time we reached the mission. I was feeling pretty good about everything we had accomplished, and I hoped my luck would continue—I just had to remember how to get back underground. Michael followed me closely, and I was certain he couldn't believe the secret passages I was able to guide him through. Ultimately, we ended up in the hallway between our two bedrooms.

"I'm way too revved up to hit the sack," I said, "Let's head to Sister Mary B.'s computer and type out what we need to send Dr. Gabel first thing in the morning. Actually, I noticed she had a fax machine next to her printer."

Michael agreed. In no time, we had put together quite a list of known kidnappers, occurrences of the past couple weeks, a proposed agenda for Wednesday's MoneyGram pick-up, a handprint from Angelo's attacker, and a shoelace found in the candle shop. We were extremely hopeful that our hard work would pay off.

"What do you think about contacting Dr. Gabel while all of this is still fresh in our minds?" I quizzed.

"Good idea," Michael said, "It's actually about 7:00 a.m. in the States, so it's a good time to call."

As he opened up his phone, he dialed in the number and handed it to me. It only took two rings for the doctor to answer.

"Hello, Carrie, I've been waiting for your call," he answered while coughing.

"Hi there, Dr. Gabel," I said, "Michael and I have gone through quite an ordeal, and we are hoping you can help us out. We would like to fax over a list of occurrences and ask whether you can steer us to the best course of action locally. We have physical proof in our possession, and we would be happy to get it to any authority figure you can name."

Within seconds, he had given me his fax number to send off our findings. I handed it to Michael and pointed to the fax machine. He then gave me the name and address of a municipal police officer right in Capri. We could take what we had obtained and hand it off to the officer.

"Carrie, please listen carefully," he said. His voice starting to fade, but he continued: "I am reading all your clever work as it comes over my fax machine now. For the safety of the children, please ask them to stay inside until this matter is resolved. Once I have called you and confirmed it is over, I have one final mission for you to complete before you return to the United States. Do you understand?"

"Yes, sir, I understand," I said, "Thank you for helping us, and I will wait to hear back from you soon."

Chapter 56

By the time I had snuggled in next to Shiloh, it didn't take me long to unwind. It actually felt as though I had been away from him for weeks, and I promised the little guy we would be heading back to our home soon.

I was awakened by Sister Mary B.'s knock on my door. I checked my watch and saw that it was only eight o'clock.

"Sister, I am just fine. I will be out in the kitchen just as soon as I put some clothes on," I said.

"Thank God, child," she said, "I have been praying both of you would return safely, and I see He has answered my prayers. Angelo and I will wait for you in the kitchen."

My eyes felt as though I had not even closed them. A quick swish with cold water solved that problem, and Shiloh and I headed over to Michael's door.

"C'mon in," he said sleepily.

"I decided if Sister Mary B. woke me up, I'd wake you up," I joked. "I'll meet you in the kitchen so we can go over everything with Angelo. Also, when do you want to head back into town to the police?"

"After we grab something to eat. I'll head into town while you tell Angelo the full story of who we really are," he said.

Ah, yes. I had forgotten I never finished my confession. It seems like a lifetime ago when I tried to explain the circumstances to him. As I turned from Michael's door, Angelo greeted me in the hallway.

"Thank goodness you both are safe," he said, "I was worried I made a mistake by not going with you. We are safe here. What more can I do to help?"

"Absolutely nothing," I said, "I have something I can do for you, however."

The three of us headed to the kitchen and grabbed some coffee and toast. Since Shiloh needed to run his little legs in the backyard, I walked Michael over to the fence. He had all of our findings in an envelope and pictures on his phone.

"Just tell our story, drop it all off, and head back, okay?" I asked. "Better yet, let me take Shiloh back inside, and I'll go with you."

"That is a better deal," Michael said, "I am certain they will need both of our testimonies before they can proceed."

I was the first one to grab onto Michael's hand as we were walking up the cobblestone path into town. My feelings for him had certainly changed since we had first met. Something told me it would normally take a lot more time to have this much trust between friends. Funny how life's circumstances change the course of a relationship.

CHAPTER 57

AFTER FINDING THE POLICEMAN Dr. Gabel had named over the phone—and after Michael and I told our story in the presence of two other officers who recorded our speech—we were told everything was in their hands. I was actually surprised to find they thanked us for all of our work. I was *not* surprised to have them tell us we put ourselves in danger and should never have done what we did. They even went as far as telling us our passports could be held if we continued to remain involved. By noon, we were given an escort back to the mission and told to stay in Italy until they gave us the go ahead on flying back to the States.

Dr. Gabel had told us to finish up and head back once things had been resolved. *It'd be such a shame not to enjoy the countryside rather than waiting inside an underground orphanage,* I thought.

"Michael, are you up for some traveling until we hear back from the local authorities?" I asked.

"Of course!" he said with a big grin, "Just what do you have in mind?"

"I grabbed some pamphlets as I came through security at the airport, and I thought we might check them out. I've heard so many good things about Venice, and Rail Europe can train us the 330 miles in one fun-filled afternoon. Any takers for yet another adventure?"

I could tell by his face that all I needed to do was take his hand to the local rail in Naples. I hoped the trip would be just what the two of us needed after all the happenings of the past few weeks. Angelo could remain at the mission to supervise the safety of the children, and we could explore more of Italy while awaiting permission from the authorities to fly back to the States.

"Go ahead and grab your backpack. I'll make Sister Mary B. and Angelo aware that we are heading to Venice via train, and I'll meet you in my room in about thirty minutes," I said.

"Fantastic," was the only word coming out of Michael's mouth.

I tried to tell myself to think about our day trip as just another mini-vacation, but as we walked through the center of Capri's shops, I just couldn't shake the feeling that we were being watched. Perhaps it was because I hadn't physically seen the authorities arrest the bad guys who had put us through so much. Or perhaps it was simply because I had seen way too many television shows in which the bad guys got away. Whatever it was, I decided to share my thoughts with Michael.

"You are being way too deep," Michael said, "The chances of those guys tailing us now are a zillion to one. Lighten up, enjoy life, and stop worrying."

"You're right. The little guy and I are the ones next to you relishing the fact that the three of us can get away without any distractions," I said. "Lead on."

We soon found our way to the tram that would be our escape from all the secret passageways of the mission church. I suddenly thought, *There is no way Mandie will believe my story. After all, she was the one who thought I was crazy for even answering Dr. Gabel's ad.* I had to smile as I thought about how her eyes would widen when I shared the mysterious door knocks, the closet escape routes, and my near discovery in the attic candle shop.

"Hey, where's your mind?" Michael quizzed.

"Sorry, I was thinking about Mandie and how she's going to think we made up so many things just to make the trip more interesting," I answered.

"No need to apologize. I'm having a hard time believing it—and I lived it!"

As we boarded the tramway, I watched Michael's eyes as he took in the beauty of the sea from Capri's cliffs. How long it must have taken to dynamite into the hillside in order to allow modern day explorers to see the beauty of the Mediterranean from high above the cliffs. Everyone in the tram cars had either their cameras or phones snapping picture after picture. I closed my eyes in an attempt to lock in the visual beauty so I could recall it later in life. If only that were possible. We proceeded straight downward, going ever so slowly. We inched by rocks and hillside flowers until finally coming to rest near where the hydrofoil had dropped thousands of travelers over the years.

"How did you come from Naples to the Isle?" I asked.

"By ferry, why?"

"Because the super fast way for us to get back to Naples would be the hydrofoil, and I was wondering if you took it," I answered. For some strange reason, I wanted this mini-trip to be one we developed together. We had both found different means of transportation over to Capri, but taking the exciting hydrofoil back as a couple seemed right.

"Hey, you're the one who found Italian soil first, I'll go on your lead," Michael said. "What is a hydrofoil anyway?"

"It's a boat with wing-like foils mounted under the hull. As it increases in speed, the hydrofoils lift the hull up and out of the water. I've been told we can go as fast as two times the wind speed. Still up for it?" I asked.

"Are you kidding? Ready and willing."

It seemed like the perfect mode of transportation, and even Shiloh's eyes never left the water that was gleaming all around us. I was able to point out the volcano Vesuvius, and in no time at all, we were approaching dry land.

"Just think of the contrast between this and sitting in a gondola in Venice," Michael said laughing. "I'm beginning to think the past is just a blur, and the present is pretty exciting." He reached down and squeezed my hand.

Surprisingly, quite a few passengers were on the boat. As we all walked along toward the narrow gate to exit, I noticed Shiloh's small body started shaking. Normally, he only shook like that when he was near someone he recognized. I knew Michael could not be the person because we'd been together for days. Once again, I started to get an uneasy feeling. Before I could think deeper, we were off the boat and walking toward the parked vehicles. Shiloh had once more relaxed, and I dismissed the thought.

Chapter 58

THE RAIL EUROPE CLERK was soon explaining all of our options. His suggestion was to purchase compartment seating. He explained that the car was separated into enclosed cabins, which opened onto a corridor along one side of the car. In first-class, cabins could accommodate up to six passengers, in second-class cabins could hold up to eight. We were told it was our lucky day because very few had purchased tickets to Venice, and we could have a cabin all to ourselves. The next train was leaving soon.

"Sold!" Michael exclaimed, and he handed the man the money.

We were told we could find any empty cabin and make it our own. It only took three tries before we located one. Once inside, we had barely gotten comfortable before we felt the train pulling out of the station. The window ledge was the perfect spot for Shiloh, and it left more than enough room for the two of us to watch as the countryside meandered by our two wide windows.

"Know what I wish?" I asked sheepishly.

"No idea."

"I wish we had six months to take in all of Europe before heading back home," I said.

"Be careful what you wish for," Michael answered laughing.

The motion of the train soon relaxed us, and it just felt right settling into each other's arms on one side of the cabin. We were living the good life. My concentration was soon broken, however, by the sound of squeaking wheels outside our door. What on earth?

"Food trolley, food trolley."

"Great," I said with eager anticipation as I opened the narrow doorway.

Evidently, we were hungry because our eyes immediately focused on sandwiches, snack bags, and cold drinks instead of the gentleman pushing the cart.

"We'll take one of each," Michael said with some humor in his voice.

Both of our hands were full, and we even had food under our arms before the sound of the food cart was off in the distance. I had never given Shiloh people food before, but I figured a few dropped chips were not worth the hassle of picking up. We both noted that we could not remember the last time we had eaten, and our goodies were soon digested.

We were, once again, settling into each other's arms when Shiloh jumped from the window ledge and found his way to the foot of the doorway. His nose was twitching, and within seconds, he started a low, deep growl. I had learned early on not to discourage his canine smells and hearing, so I got down on the floor next to him.

"What's going on, little guy?" I whispered.

At that point, I started hearing something. My first thought was that travelers were walking by. My second thought was not as innocent.

"Michael," I whispered, "I think someone is standing outside our door trying to listen in."

Shiloh's low growl continued, and Michael soon was on the floor with me. He shook his head and put his fingers to his lips to motion to me to stop talking. I watched as he tilted his chin sideways and touched his face to the floor in an attempt to look under the door. His up and down head shake, let me know that someone was standing just outside. I felt alarmed. *Why would someone be standing still outside our door?* Michael's hand slowly reached upward and, ever so gently, he turned the lock on the doorknob. The slight sound must have alerted the person because we heard footsteps walk away. Shiloh stopped growling and went back to the window ledge.

As he helped me up, Michael attempted to mask his look. I, however, still had the hairs standing up on the back of my arms.

"Must have been the wrong cabin," Michael said calmly.

"Or," I said, still whispering, "it was the right cabin, and we are being followed."

CHAPTER 59

THE CONCLUSION OF OUR train ride was uneventful, and Shiloh slept until we pulled into the station. We both had read through the many Venice brochures, and we had come up with our top ten things to see. We smiled as we read each other's list. On the top of both of our lists was wandering aimlessly through the streets and alleys for the first couple of hours. We read that we could find Venice's many charming and often-empty squares to our liking, and we thought it would be the very best way to acclimate ourselves to the city's hidden beauty.

As we exited the train—and after walking just a few feet—I couldn't help but turn around. I guess I needed the reassurance that I wouldn't recognize anyone. All I really saw was lots and lots of people. I tried to look for specifics (like facial hair), but everyone seemed to blend in. As I turned back around, I noticed Michael was also checking behind us. I didn't think he was convincing when he told me he didn't believe we were being followed.

"Satisfied we don't have company?" I asked.

"Relax. It's just the two of us and Shiloh," he answered. "You're trying to bring way too much drama into this day trip. Let's get started by finding an outside table for two and ordering some wine and crackers."

To our surprise and amazement, we had scarcely gotten off the train before we were escorted onto one of Venice's water-buses. *Oh my gosh, water was everywhere!*

"Can you believe we were so busy thinking about things to do that we forgot Venice was a city of water?" I asked, laughing out loud.

"Now this is a perfect beginning to check out the sights and sounds of this unique city," Michael said.

I thought everyone on the water-bus was a first-time traveler to Italy because, as I looked around, everyone's eyes were slowly moving back and forth as if at a tennis match. We just could not take it all in. I did overhear one of the women say that the number one Vaporetto water-bus would be the ideal way to tour the Grand Canal. She said it was actually the equivalent to a city bus tour.

We soon found ourselves stepping out into quite a large piazza. The more we walked and window shopped, the more relaxed I became. In no time, we found the perfect setting to share some merlot and enjoy the outside of St. Mark's Basilica. *What person would not find the onion domes and multicolored marble pillars breathtaking to look at over some wine and sunshine?* I wondered. We overheard many tourists walking by our table. They talked about the inside of the church and how it had many floor-to-ceiling mosaics. I told Michael that if we didn't have time to tour, we needed to stop in to say a prayer. I hadn't shared why I felt that need, but as we sat overlooking the magnificent structure, I decided to give it my best shot.

"Michael, I thought I'd share a short reason why I find myself almost obligated to enter into a first-time church and say a prayer. When I was a child, my mother would tell me that, anytime we were on vacation and entering a new church, I could say a short prayer and make a wish. Of course, the wish was the motivation, and after mother shared her story with me, I jumped at the chance to find new churches. My wishes were pretty small back in those days, and I truly don't remember any of them going unanswered."

"So that's the rationale behind it," Michael said laughing, "Let's hope all your wishes continue to be answered here in Venice."

We both raised our glasses for a toast, and out of the blue, Shiloh leaped from my lap and was heading off into the piazza chasing after one of the many pigeons. It took us both by surprise, and within seconds, we were up on our feet.

"Shiloh!" I yelled, "Come!"

"You head to the right," Michael said loudly, "I'll go left to head him off."

I found myself running around tourists and the many tables set up in the piazza. Nothing mattered but getting the little guy back into my arms. I still had my eyes on him as he continued to dart after each and every bird before they flew into the warm air. I watched as his little body rounded the corner of St. Mark's and disappeared. In seconds, I was turning the corner myself. Just then, I saw a thin-built man reach down and scoop him up.

"Sir! Sir!" I yelled, "That is *my* puppy. Please hold on to him for me."

What happened next actually stunned me. His eyes met mine, and I immediately sensed anger. In one fleeting second, he laid an envelope on the ground, turned, and took off running.

"Shiloh! Shiloh!" I continued yelling. I found myself standing over the envelope.

Oh my God, it has my name printed on the front of it! In the short time it took me to look down to the ground and then back up, the man and my dog were gone.

"Carrie! Carrie!" Michael shouted as he ran up beside me, out of breath. "I've lost him."

"A man just took him! I just saw a man reach down and take him, Michael."

I reached down, grabbed the envelope, and started running in the direction I had last seen the man and Shiloh. I heard Michael's footsteps behind me, and in no time, he was running next to me.

"Look for a man wearing a dark blue shirt and jeans," I shouted.

So many people and so much activity, I thought, It just could not be possible for this man to disappear. Who would want a dog so badly he would steal one? I wanted, in the worst way, to stop and read the envelope with my name on it, but I knew our action now would be the only chance at finding Shiloh before he blended into the hundreds of tourists. I was not about to let my worst fears override the chance at catching the crazy person.

We ran for the better half of an hour. Michael kept up with me, and he never once questioned my motive. He knew how special my dog was to me, and he also knew we could not leave Venice until we found him.

"I think we've lost him," I said, tears streaming down my cheeks.

"Carrie, we'll find him. I promise you, we'll find him. What was the piece of paper you picked up on the ground back there?"

"Please, Michael, hold me. You really think we will find a small dog in this huge city? He doesn't even know how to swim. He hates the water. Why would someone want to take my dog anyway?" I questioned, collapsing in his arms.

"Carrie, listen to me. What was the paper you picked up off the ground?"

As reality set in, I pulled back from his arms and reached into my vest for the envelope with my name on it. I handed it to Michael. I noticed his eyes getting big as he read the words out loud: "To the American girl, Carrie." I watched as he gently pulled the flap open and brought out a small, crinkled piece of paper. I wiped away the tears from my eyes and went to stand next to him. We both read in silence: *Hotel Gambero. We will contact you.*

CHAPTER 60

T HE HOTEL ANTICA LOCANDA al Gambero took three minutes by foot from the piazza San Marco. We actually had no idea whether it was the same hotel the crinkled piece of paper was referring to. As we walked into the lobby and found a desk clerk, we soon learned we were in the right hotel—more specifically, they confirmed their hotel had the same name as the one printed on the paper.

After discussing the pros and cons of checking in, we decided it was the only logical choice to make if we ever hoped to get Shiloh back. The one fear we both had continued to loom over our decision: what if we had gone to the wrong hotel?

To ensure my presence was completely known, I checked in using as many references as I could to being American. I wanted to ensure that the clerks at the front desk knew that the *American girl, Carrie,* was a registered guest.

Once we got to our room, we both looked at each other and collapsed onto the bed. I knew we had to think about what had happened. *How did we not see this coming? What on earth made us think we could venture out of Capri and assume we would not be followed? Why are these men obsessed with making our lives so miserable?* The answer was simple: Angelo took their money away, and they wanted to get even.

"Didn't the Italian authorities say they were handling everything?" quizzed Michael.

"I thought so. Guess that assumption was wrong. The scary thing about all of this is that we knew going into it that they kidnapped Angelo's brother and planned on extorting monies. What on earth made us think they wouldn't resort to foul play yet again?"

"You know," said Michael, "this is just the beginning of their demands. They are going to hold Shiloh over our heads until they come up with some other ultimatum for us."

"It's not like we're rich," I said. I started to cry again.

"Carrie, they don't know we have no money. They think we are all rich Americans who can and will pay to have a loved one returned," he answered.

Michael rolled on his side and wiped the tears off my cheeks. He gathered me in his arms and held me tight. My thoughts raced to how far I would go to get Shiloh back. Those dang men didn't know how tough I was. They had no idea that Shiloh and I were survivors—and fate had placed us together. I would definitely not give up on the little guy. I just hoped they were ready for all heck to break loose before I left Italian soil without him.

CHAPTER 61

THE ONE THING ABOUT being prisoners in a hotel room was that we had lots and lots of time to talk. Because we knew we had to hang around until we heard from someone (either by paper or phone), Michael and I opened our windows and soaked in the warmth of our first day and night in Venice. Unable to sleep—and not yet wanting to venture down into the hotel's restaurant for fear we might miss some information about Shiloh—we bought our own bottle of wine and some sandwiches, and we started reminiscing about our first encounter back in the States.

"I remember, like yesterday, when you moved into our apartment complex. I actually enjoyed guessing what your profession might be. I first thought you were an attorney or stock broker because you always carried a briefcase. However, I gave up on that thought because I never seemed to see you in a business suit. And then I guessed you might have something to do with sports equipment because you were always taking football, baseball, or tennis gear out of your trunk," I said to him. "And," I emphasized, "you were always in shorts and a T-shirt."

"So you actually noticed what I was wearing whenever you saw me?" Michael asked, starting to laugh.

"Well, duh, of course!" I said. "I also noticed how good looking you were, and that's why I decided you might play sports for a living. You know, like a pro something or other. Of course, I secretly hoped you were a male model for GQ," I said, hitting his arm.

"So tell me: how did you find out what I really do for a living?"

"I asked the neighbor who parks next to your car when I returned home one day," I answered. I had a big grin on my face.

"And did I pass the test of doing something honorable for a living?"

"Yes, yes, you did," I answered. "You'll have to admit that I was fairly close, but I probably wouldn't have nailed it on my own. After all, being a sports writer for a major magazine is a bit out of the box, so to speak."

The entire time I was talking, I hadn't really noticed Michael's hand playing with my long hair. His finger was encircling one of my locks. His eyes watched my lips, and when I stopped speaking, he leaned over and kissed me. I kissed him back. I didn't even have to think about it. I reacted as quickly as if it were expected, which it wasn't. I felt as though I were having one of those out-of-body experiences people have written about. You know, the kind where the person is having surgery and leaves his body to hover above everyone in the operating room. I watched myself looking down, and I saw both of my hands reach up to hold his face. I simply did not want the experience to end.

I sensed he felt the same as he pulled me closer and put his arms around my shoulders and back. *What a perfect blend of a firm yet gentle touch,* I thought. We laid next to each other for several minutes. Nothing needed to be said. His lips finally left mine and found my forehead. His kisses erased any doubts I had. I found myself mesmerized as I felt his nearness first on my cheek and then on my earlobe.

"You know," I whispered, "this isn't very fair."

"How so?" he whispered back.

"Because you are attempting to take advantage of someone mourning the loss of her best friend. I am especially vulnerable at this very moment," I answered, gently pushing his arms away from my body.

"I would never attempt to take advantage of you, Carrie," Michael replied, "Matter of fact—"

The loud knock came as a surprise to both of us, and for a fleeting moment, I actually waited for Shiloh to start barking. Michael was up and off the bed in no time. He headed for the door, but he didn't get five feet from the bed before we both noticed another envelope. It had been slipped under the door. In one fluid motion, he bent down to pick it up and opened the door.

"No one," he uttered as he closed the door. "This has your name on it, again."

He walked over to the bed with envelope in hand and placed it on the spread next to me. It was the same writing, the same words: *To the American girl, Carrie.*

"I can't open it," I said, starting to cry. "You do it."

Without hesitation, he tore open the envelope and read out loud: "Gondolier Donato at Rialto bridge, tomorrow night, eight o'clock."

CHAPTER 62

Two thoughts came to mind after Michael read the short note. The first was how furious I was that they were making me wait yet another day before I could hold my dog. The second thought racing into my mind came out at a high volume: "How dare they dictate where we need to be at a certain time!"

"Carrie, calm down. Let's think this one out," Michael answered.

I fell back down on the bed, and for one fleeting moment, I felt defeated. *How dare they take something I love so dearly and hold it over my head. Why am I in the middle of this anyway? What kind of mess have I gotten myself into? Please, dear God, protect Shiloh and help us come up with the strategy to get him back safely.*

"I just said a prayer, Michael, and I am starting to think calmly again."

"Great," he said. "The good news is, we found the right hotel. We now know how to get the little guy back into your arms."

"We do?" I questioned.

"Yes. We will work on a plan for tomorrow night, and I promise that I will rescue the little guy," Michael pledged. "Now, enough of you being so sad. Head into the shower first, and I'll call down to make a couple reservations in the restaurant."

The warm water pouring over my head and body was just what I needed to make my outlook positive again. As I stood under the shower, I thought back on the tender kisses Michael had given me. *What on earth would I have done without him coming to my rescue in Capri and Venice? We are a great team together, and he does seem to have strengths that complement my weaknesses.*

As I dried off, I noticed the light above starting to flicker. A smile came to my face as I reached for my tote and pulled out my devotional. "Through briers, through waste places through glades, up mountain heights, down into valleys, I lead. But ever with the leadership goes the Helping Hand. I am beside you. Can you not feel my presence? Contact with Me is not gained by the senses. Spirit-consciousness replaces sight."

My thoughts were interrupted by Michael knocking on the door and telling me we had fifteen minutes to get down to the restaurant before they closed the kitchen. As we hurriedly found our way down two flights of stairs, we were pleasantly surprised to be directed through the dining room and into a small square (a *campiello*) at the foot of a bridge for outside dining.

"What a beautiful, picturesque setting! And the candles make it even more charming. How much did you have to bribe the management for this wonderful table?"

"Not one red cent. They must have thought we needed some serenity just by looking at us," he answered and smiled.

The warm night air was exhilarating, and it gave us the perfect setting to wind down and plot our next course of action. As we talked back and forth, I could tell Michael was determined to rescue Shiloh and bring everything to a dramatic halt.

"Remember," I said, "we won't know how many of *them* will be by this particular gondola."

"Do you actually think *they* have men all over Italy?" Michael questioned. "I doubt it. We have been told to find a particular gondolier for a reason. The only logical thought is that they want control of the situation. I say we go in with both guns blazing and grab the dog."

"The only problem there is that we don't have guns to blaze," I answered. "Have you ever been in a fight in your life?"

"You don't give me a whole lot of credit," he answered.

"Hey, I'm just trying to consider all of our options," I said. "Am I to understand you will be using your fists while I use my incredibly fast reflexes to grab the dog?"

"Once we assess the situation to see just how many are involved, we can react accordingly."

"Maybe we should, once again, bring in the local authorities," I commented.

"And tell them what? We don't have any papers stating Shiloh is yours. They haven't asked for any sum of money, and all we really know for certain is that Shiloh ran after some pigeons."

"Okay, we do it your way," I said, nodding my head. "I guess we are the only two people who actually believe these thugs are threatening us because they are hacked we turned their scheme in to the police back in Capri."

CHAPTER 63

WE BOTH FELT LIKE we should choose traditional Venetian dishes, but the choices were still mind-boggling. The head chef ventured outside in the night air to help us decide by allowing us to sample his specialties. After hearing we were from the United States, he even brought out one of their fine wines and joined us at the table. "One day," he shared, "I want to live in New York and become a chef for one of the many fine restaurants there." He so loved being able to communicate in English, and he jumped at any and every opportunity.

We shared that we had an entire day to check out Venice, and he suggested that we go to Murano, an island in the Venetian Lagoon, for their glassblowing displays. We thanked him for his advice, but we knew we couldn't risk traveling to yet another island when we had an appointment not far from our hotel later in the day. I was really beginning to miss Shiloh, and I certainly didn't cherish the thought of arriving late at the designated bridge. He did share the location of a local glassblower, however, and we told him we might take his advice.

We could have talked for many more hours, but we could see from the waitstaff that it was well past the restaurant's normal operating hours. Evidently the chef felt a connection with us, because our meal was on the house. All he asked was that we exchange phone numbers in the event that he was successful at securing an interview in New York. I complimented him on the cover of the menu, and he graciously handed me one to keep for later framing. The hour was late, and we headed up the stairs to our much-needed room.

Once inside, I declared dibs on the bed. Michael looked around the room and saw only a small love seat. We both knew instantly that the only alternative was the floor. Both of our faces showed the look of rejection.

"Okay, what about this thought: we do the remake of *It Happened One Night* with Clark Gable," I said.

"I have absolutely no idea what you are talking about," he answered.

"You must be kidding. Are you telling me you have never seen that award-winning movie?" I quizzed.

"You hit the nail on the head."

"Let me show you rather than tell you," I said and headed over to the bedspread.

I took off the bedspread and placed it on the chair. I then grabbed the clothesline out of my tote and checked the room for hanging pictures. I took the oil painting behind the bed off the wall, and I walked across the room to the opposite side. Again, I removed the picture. With the skills I learned from reading my brother's Boy Scouts book, I promptly made two sailor knots and attached the clothesline. I then reached for the spread on the chair and draped it over the line.

"Voilà! Instant privacy for two people on one king-sized bed," I exclaimed.

I thought Michael would never stop laughing. He reached over and gave me a big bear hug. As if on cue, we both flopped down on each side of the bed and fell asleep within minutes.

CHAPTER 64

I JUST WASN'T USED to it. Shiloh always laid beside me, and not feeling his body warmth during the night made for many hours of tossing and turning. By the time I awoke, I could smell the cappuccino Michael had brought up from the lobby of the hotel. It teased my senses, and I finally opened my eyes to see Michael sitting on the side of the bed, watching me and holding the cup.

"How long have you been here?" I asked with a smile on my face.

"Only a minute or two. Kind of fun waking up with you in the same room. How did you sleep?"

"Not great," I answered, "I'll sleep much better after we get this over with tonight. What does our day hold?"

"I was thinking we could check out the glassblowing shop and the Rialto bridge before tonight. Are you up for it?"

"Willing and able," I said. "Just give me a few minutes to throw water on my face and brush my teeth, and we are out of here. Hand me one of those pastries you brought up, pretty please."

"Hey, I'll hand you one of these if you promise to keep a smile on your face today."

"It's a deal," I said, leaning over to kiss him. "I'll meet you down in the lobby in fifteen minutes."

By the time I spotted Michael in the lobby, he had already found a map and was checking it out with pen in hand.

"Both of our chosen destinations aren't very far from here, so do you want to check out the glass shop first?" he questioned.

As I nodded in agreement, he reached for my hand. We set off on our next adventure. The sights and sounds of mid-morning Venice were indescribable. Shop owners swept their entryways, tourists started to mingle, and the smell of the Mediterranean filled our nostrils.

"There it is," Michael said, pointing toward several shops down the street. "The glassblower is actually working outside his shop, and people are starting to gather."

He was right. We walked closer, and I was in awe as I watched him form glass into whatever his calling was for the day. He actually had several tables set up with beautiful configurations that he had formed earlier. My eyes caught the one thing I knew I wanted to purchase. It was a beautiful blown glass Madonna and Child framed on red velvet. I thought it would look quite lovely on my wall next to the framed menu from the restaurant where we ate last night.

Michael chose a handsome lighthouse in Murano as his keepsake, and the two of us continued admiring the artwork for over an hour. We almost felt guilty about shopping while Shiloh was being held captive somewhere.

"Ready to hike over to scan the site of the Rialto bridge?" Michael asked.

"Yes," I said excitedly, "I can't wait to check out the area where we will be rescuing the little guy."

CHAPTER 65

MICHAEL WAS RIGHT: OUR walk to find the bridge didn't take as long as I thought it might. We soon found ourselves in the middle of numerous tourists standing in line to rent gondolas. The amount of people mingling was welcome because we wanted to blend in and not be obvious about our motives. You could tell by Michael's eyes that he was intent on designing a plan for our upcoming night. I walked next to him and saw him checking the distance across the bridge and the length of each gondola.

"Look," I said, "each boat has a specific name on it. I wonder how we will ever begin to find the name of the right gondolier."

"Looks like we will just have to start asking around when we get here tonight," he answered.

"I've really been thinking about this a lot," I said. "What will they want in exchange for giving Shiloh back to us? They aren't just going to hand him over, right?"

"These are bad guys, Carrie. They are going to ask for money probably. They may not even have the dog with them tonight. We are just going to have to play along with them. But if Shiloh is with them, he *will* be in your arms again before we go back to the hotel tonight. I promise you that."

I decided to check out a few things while Michael was off doing his surveillance work. I took the shortest gondola line and made small talk with the couple in front of me. By the time I got to the front of the line, I was able to ask about the cost for a night's ride. It was a great deal higher than I had imagined, but I knew that we would have to buy a ticket.

"Looks like there will be plenty of people, and I've even spotted a local policeman who seems to be patrolling around the boats," Michael said. "I can't imagine anyone doing us harm with so much activity."

"Good," I said, "I feel better already."

"It looks as though these boats seat as many as six people," Michael said. "That answers why there are so many tourists hanging around. It's almost like an amusement park ride with about three boats pulling up every five minutes or so. I say the more people, the better."

"Do you think we should check around and find the specific gondolier mentioned in the note?" I asked.

"Not really. I'd rather have it all go down tonight at eight—like the note said."

I suggested we head over the bridge to the Rialto market and check out the locals at the fruit, vegetable, and fish stands that had been there for centuries. As we crossed over the bridge, the views were incredible. Everyone had their cameras out. I reached for mine, yelled at Michael to turn around, and quickly snapped a picture.

We soon found our way to stall after stall of produce and fish.

"Oh my gosh!" I exclaimed, "The fish is so fresh! It doesn't even smell fishy."

Within minutes, we were buying one of just about everything in sight. The produce looked as though it had just been picked, and we found ourselves eating to our hearts' content. We were only about one-third of the way down the marketplace when I heard a small dog barking.

"Michael, do you hear that?"

"I hear a lot of things right now. What particular sound are you referring to?"

"That dog barking. It's almost like Shiloh whining," I answered.

We stood perfectly still, allowing only our heads to move from side to side. It was really hard to block out all the tourist noises and concentrate solely on the sound of a small dog. It was really hard, but we both did it. The two of us ended up facing a small, wooden fish stand. We could see a young woman from the waist up. She was bending up and down, attempting to push something or someone off of her legs.

I seized Michael's hand, and we started walking toward the stand (and the sound of the whining). We must have had an odd look on our faces because she locked eyes with me and instantly reached down to pick up a small dog. When she turned, she suddenly started running from the stand. *Was it possible? Was she holding Shiloh in her arms? And if not, why would she be running away from us?*

"I don't know about you," Michael yelled, "but I think we should attempt to catch her."

"Fine with me," I replied, "I'm with you!"

We soon found ourselves running in and around dozens of wooden sheds set up to sell the catches and produce of the day. It helped tremendously that we could see glimpses of her red top. I was able to keep up with Michael's zigzagging mainly because of my adrenaline rush. Our two sets of eyes allowed us to keep her in our sights, and as we got closer and closer, Michael let go of my hand. He was able to extend his long reach to her arm.

"Stop!" he yelled as he turned her around with one frantic twist.

We both stood there staring at a young woman wearing a bright red top. Her eyes showed how frightened she was, and she was out of breath. That, however, was not what caught our attention—the fact that she had no dog in her arms was the shock.

"*Mi scusi,*" Michael said, looking directly at her. "English?"

"*Si,*" she answered, out of breath.

"Where is the dog?" he asked.

"No dog," she replied.

The minute she answered, my mind flashed back to seeing her for the first time at the wooden fish stand. I was certain she picked up a small dog before she started to run. *If that was the case,* I thought, *where was the dog now?*

"We lost my dog and thought you might have him," I broke in.

"No dog, no dog," she replied.

I had always been good at reading faces, and I thought, *Either she did not have a dog in her arms, or she is really good at deceiving us.* The more I looked at her face, the more defeated I felt. I was so sure we were right, and yet she looked so honest.

"*Scusa,*" Michael said, letting go of her arm.

The moment he let her go, she turned and walked off into the crowded marketplace.

"Did you believe her?" I quizzed.

"We were forced to believe her. She didn't have Shiloh in her arms. But no, I think she was lying to us," he answered. "Hopefully we haven't screwed things up for tonight."

CHAPTER 66

I'M CERTAIN MICHAEL SAW the disappointment on my face. It was pretty hard not to be down. We were both hoping for a better ending to all of our running around the marketplace. As we headed back over the bridge, we held onto the fact that things could only get better.

"We tried," Michael said, reaching over to give me a hug.

"I know," I answered. "I hope tonight will have a happier ending."

We continued walking and soon found outdoor tables with bottles of wine set up. It looked very inviting after our hike up and down the Rialto Bridge. By the time we placed our order for some fresh seafood, the afternoon sun was behind the buildings, allowing us some much-needed shade." I can't think of a better place to spend time with you," Michael said with a smile.

"That's a relief," I answered.

"Don't suppose I could talk you into hiking back to the hotel after this meal and cuddling up with me on the bed?" he asked

"I don't really think you will have to twist my arm," I said, reaching for his hand.

CHAPTER 67

THE MINUTE WE REACHED our room, I went to the hanging bedspread and pulled it off of the clothesline. I pushed Michael onto the bed, and we both found ourselves laughing and acting like teenagers.

"How about a foot massage in lieu of cuddling?" I asked.

"Deal," he replied as he turned my body around so my head was at the foot of the bed.

"My feet are killing me, and I promise you a great cuddle after the pain subsides," I said.

Michael had just begun rubbing my feet when his cell phone made a noise. We both looked at each other with the same concern. *Who would be sending him a text message?*

"You aren't going to believe this," he said and handed me his cell.

He was right: I didn't believe it. I actually had to read it twice before I responded.

"How did they get your cell number?" I questioned.

"The only people I have given my number to are the Capri authorities. Your guess is as good as mine."

"Kind of creepy, don't you think?" I asked.

"Just makes me want to get back to the States where security feels tighter," he answered.

"The more I think about all of this, the more I think we should head to the police here in Venice to file a stolen dog report," I said. "We need something to fall back on if this doesn't go down right tonight."

"Okay, you've probably got a good thought there," Michael said. "Make sure you have the envelope and note so we can show them some proof."

I got up from the bed and started to walk over to my tote bag on the dresser. I detected something partially pushed under the door. I reached down, pulled a note from the envelope, and read it out loud: "No *polizia* or we *danni piccolo cane.*" As I was reading it to Michael, I grabbed my airport translation book and researched. "No police or we harm small dog."

My eyes welled up, and I sat down in the middle of the floor. I pulled Shiloh's blue collar out of the envelope and held his dog tags in my shaking hand.

"How dare they tell us what we can or cannot do to get Shiloh back," I said tearfully.

Michael's jaw was clenched, and he came to sit beside me on the floor. His arms made me feel like I was wrapped in a cocoon, and we just sat there for a minute without another word.

"Somehow I'm beginning to think they have connections with the authorities locally. We should just stick to our plan tonight and leave the cops out of this," he finally said.

"Fine, but where are we going to get the money they want us to bring?" I quizzed.

"Two can play this game, and we don't even have to find a bank to make this deal work," he answered.

CHAPTER 68

A GREAT DEAL OF the afternoon was spent mainly in silence, and I turned down several of Michael's suggestions to walk my sadness off in the marketplace. When the maid knocked on our door, we both welcomed the interruption. Her constant knocking, however, had us concerned. Rather than saying *entrare,* I rushed to open the door for her.

I was not prepared for what I saw. There, on the door, was a big, red circle with a cross through it. The shocking part was the blood used was still dripping on the floor. The maid's eyes met mine, and we both stared at the door in disbelief. She was mumbling something over and over in Italian and attempting to sop the blood off the carpet.

"Oh my God, Michael, come over here!" I yelled.

He rushed my way and stopped right in front of the door.

"Whoa," he said and stepped back. "What on earth is this all about?"

The maid must have understood English because she answered him immediately: "This is the mark of a local gang." Her lips were quivering as she continued, "It means you and your family are targeted."

"Targeted?" Michael asked, "Targeted for what?"

"For something bad to happen, *Signore,*" she answered.

As the maid continued soaking up the dripping blood, I needed to ask the question on my mind: "Miss, where does one get this much blood?"

Her eyes looked down. She kept washing the door with her wet towel, but she did not answer. I looked at Michael, and he repeated the same question. No answer. As she stood up from kneeling, her eyes met mine.

"I am so sorry to tell you, but this much blood usually comes from a small animal. Like a pig," she added as an afterthought.

"A pig?" I questioned, "Does it ever come from a family's dog or cat?"

"*Si,*" she answered, "sometimes."

I actually felt my stomach start to ache. *Please, dear Lord, don't let this be Shiloh's blood.* As I turned to head into our bathroom to grab a wet towel, Michael followed. He turned me around and held me tight against his chest.

"Do not—I repeat—do not think the worst," he said. "Whoever these people are, they are trying to scare us. Do not let them win. Think positive. We will get Shiloh back tonight."

His words brought me back to reality. *He is right. I should not assume anything with these horrible men. I, too, believe they are trying to scare us. I will never let them know it's working.* I quickly grabbed my camera and took a picture as further evidence.

CHAPTER 69

B Y THE TIME THE ugly smattering of blood was washed off our hotel door and the maid had gone, I felt more composed. I was especially thankful that no other guests witnessed the lengthy cleanup. I found myself thinking how gutsy the person must have been to paint the door while we were inside the room. I knew gangs existed in the States, but I had no idea to what extent they existed in Italy.

"The more I think about it," I said, "the more I think it was not a local gang. I think it was our bullies attempting to make it look that way."

"I thought that too, but I also think it might have been a local gang all along. You did tell me these men all had the same tattoo, right?" he questioned.

"Right," I answered. "I told the local authorities everything. Wouldn't you think they would tell us if it was gang related?"

"Not really. They don't owe us any explanation."

"Do you still feel we are safe for tonight's undertaking?" I asked.

"You must be reading my mind. I was just going over that in my thoughts. I think I'll bring along my dad's old pocket knife—just in case."

"Gee, that's the extent of keeping us safe?" I asked sarcastically.

"I guess I could attempt to buy a hand gun," Michael countered.

"Don't be silly," I said, "I certainly don't want us involved in some physical confrontation."

"Good, me either," he said. "Let's go down to the lobby and gather up all the newspapers we can. I have a project for the two of us before we head out later tonight."

I was in no mood to question him. I followed him down the stairs to the main part of the hotel. We found ourselves at the front desk, and it didn't take long before our arms were full of old newspapers. I had no idea what his intentions were, and it further surprised me when he asked for a couple pairs of scissors and lots of rubber bands. He could tell by the look on my face how crazy I thought he was, and my expression didn't change until he explained himself inside our room.

"Okay, here's the deal:" he said, "we need to make it look as though we have a great deal of money. The only way I know to do that is to put paper in between the top and bottom bills."

"Excellent thought," I said. "Very, very clever. I'm up for the task."

The two of us sat for well over two hours cutting up the newspapers and placing the bundles into one of my spare tote bags. It surprised me how real it all appeared—and how heavy the bag was once we finished.

With our cutting complete, we walked outside to the closest restaurant. We had a delicious meal, mostly in silence. It was as though we were preparing ourselves for an Olympic event—both of trying to stay focused. I couldn't help but worry. So much could go wrong. *Please, dear Lord, protect and guide us tonight as we attempt to get Shiloh back.*

CHAPTER 70

WE COULDN'T HELP BUT notice the differences around the bridge compared to earlier in the day. Where were all the tourists? Night completely changed the appearance of things. Even the lines waiting for gondolas had condensed into a single line. My eyes were hoping to catch sight of any policemen, but I didn't have any luck. Low lighting made it difficult to see facial features, and the bridge steps that were once busy and occupied were empty. "I'm not big on this scene," I said, grabbing Michael's arm.

"It'll be all right," he answered, "Just stay close to me."

I noticed Michael shifting the tote bag to his inside hand, and I felt his arm tensing up. He might give the outward appearance of cool and collected, but his body tenseness gave me a very different vibe. It was 7:45, and I wasn't sure whether I wanted to just stand around until the appointed hour. I tugged at Michael's arm and directed him to walk with me to the shadows of a huge tree. My night vision was starting to return, and I was hoping to feel safer in the darkness.

Both of us digested the entire scene from left to right. We whispered to one another each time we suspected anything (and certainly any time we thought we saw the figure of a small dog). If I hadn't asked earlier about the gondolas running at night, I would have the impression that they were not for hire. The only proof of any activity was a young girl in the ticket stand, highlighted by a low-wattage bulb. She seemed to be listening to music through earphones.

One of my favorite getaways was San Antonio's Riverwalk, and I was hoping some of the same ambiance would transcend the fear I was feeling. The night air was calm, and the sweet smell of mimosa was everywhere. As we stood still in the shadows, a gondola slowly came into partial view on the water. Ever so serenely, it crept up closer and closer to the pavement. The only passenger was a woman holding something very close to her breast. The gondolier's head seemed to be moving back and forth at an accelerated rate as they neared the stand. It was as if he were looking for someone. We both thought he was our man.

As the boat pulled up and stopped, we were able to get a better view of his only passenger. The flickering lights overhead allowed us to see the woman's face clearly. I tried not to gasp as her facial features were revealed.

"Oh my gosh! It's the woman we chased this afternoon in the market!" I whispered.

"And just look what she's holding next to her," Michael said.

I had been so focused on the woman's face, I hadn't even noticed the small ball of fluff in her arms. It was Shiloh, alive and well—and just waiting to be rescued.

"This looks fairly easy," Michael said. "Two of them and two of us. Let's watch them for another minute and make sure things stay quiet."

We stayed hidden and focused on the situation before us. We could see no other tourists attempting to rent a gondola, and the young woman in the stand was oblivious to anything other than the book she was reading and the music she was listening to. Perhaps it was going to be as easy as it looked.

CHAPTER 71

"I SAY WE GO for it," Michael whispered, looking me in the eyes.

"Okay," I answered, "let's do it fast, very fast."

The two of us exposed ourselves and started walking over to the gondola. For some reason, I felt it showed more strength to walk without holding hands, and I released mine from Michael's before we were seen. It certainly didn't take long before Shiloh became aware of the two people walking up to the boat. He instantly started fidgeting and whining, and the young woman was having a hard time controlling him.

"Are you Donato?" Michael asked, looking only at the gondolier.

"*Si,*" he answered, "come sit in the boat."

Michael looked at me, took my hand, and helped me into the swaying gondola. I was now sitting directly across from Shiloh, and he was jumping up and down on the woman's lap.

"Shiloh, it's all right," I said quietly, "Be a good boy and sit still."

My concentration was broken when Donato asked Michael the inevitable question: "Did you bring the money?"

"Of course. It is here with me now," Michael answered. "I will hand it over to you as we reach for the dog, yes?"

"No," Donato responded adamantly, "I need to see the money before anyone reaches for anything in this boat."

Michael slowly stood up and passed the tote bag over to the gondolier. *Please, dear Lord, let him believe all the money is real.* We watched him reach into the bag and carefully bring out one of our bundles. The next several minutes were a blur.

The woman holding Shiloh unexpectedly jumped up, tossed the dog at me, bounded out onto the pavement, and started running. As she did, the gondola was pushed back into the middle of the canal. This, in turn, caused the boat to sway back and forth. Donato fell hard against the oar, and the bundle in his hand broke loose from the rubber band. Newspaper went flying

155

everywhere, and our deception was soon realized. With a knife in one hand and our bag in the other, Donato leapt onto the two of us. Michael pushed me down on the floor of the gondola before he landed on us. The next thing I heard was Michael yelling in pain, and the two of them fell out of the boat and into the water.

"Michael!" I yelled, "Are you all right?!"

The sound of splashing in the murky water was all around me, and because of the darkness, I couldn't see enough to even begin to help. Shiloh was barking louder than I had ever heard before, and the boat was rocking so much I needed to sit down in an attempt to steady it.

"Carrie!" Michael finally yelled as his head came to the surface of the water, "Get out of here … now!"

"I'm not leaving, Michael!" I screamed back, hearing more thrashing in the water.

"Go away!" Michael said more weakly.

My survival mode must have kicked into gear after hearing Michael's second plea because I grabbed the oar and attempted to row away from the commotion in the water. *Thank you, God, for my canoe training at camp years ago.* Minutes passed, and I could no longer hear the two of them. I found my way to another wide pavement area on the opposite side of the canal where I could tie up the bulky gondola. I knew I needed to get away from the area, and I said a quick prayer in which I asked for guidance back to the hotel.

Prayer does work, I thought. Shiloh and I were soon running up the narrow path toward our hotel. We took the steps two at a time to our second-floor room. We were both wet and exhausted, but at least we were safe. That was more than I could say about poor Michael.

I could not help but think about how he had kept his promise to me. Shiloh *was* in my arms for the night.

CHAPTER 72

I KNEW WHAT I had to do. I went around the room gathering all the evidence, and placed it—along with my camera and both of our passports—in my purse. So much had happened in such a short period of time since we had arrived in Venice. I made sure I had the person's name we had talked to in Capri at the police station, grabbed Shiloh, and headed downstairs to speak with the clerk.

It took two different men, but I finally found one who spoke fairly good English. After explaining that I needed directions to the nearest police station, I was told the best way to get there was by taxi—not by walking alone at night. He certainly didn't have to convince me, and in no time, I was waiting in the front of the hotel for transportation to arrive. I knew every minute with Michael missing was crucial, and my adrenaline was still racing as I shuffled back and forth until the cab arrived.

The small taxi, winding in and out of traffic, got my mind racing. *How would I present the past forty-eight hours to the authorities?* It was also at that time that I started weighing whether I should call Dr. Gabel. I was definitely beginning to feel that I was in over my head, and I could not stop thinking about Michael's yell before he hit the water. I know the knife Donato brought out in the open surprised us both, and I could only assume the blade penetrated some part of Michael's body. My worst fear kept creeping into my mind, and the only thing putting it on the back burner were the prayers I kept reciting.

Once we arrived at the station, the taxi driver was nice enough to escort me to the door. We had to walk past several intoxicated men. As we reached the top of the steps, I thanked him for his help. I must have looked pretty pathetic because he kept asking me whether I was all right. Even though my outward appearance gave the impression I was not doing too well, I did think to ask him to wait for me. I sent him back to his car so I could speak with an officer.

Evidently, the night had brought out other offenders. The small room was busting at the seams, and I was shown to an obscure corner and told someone would be with me soon. After ten minutes, I walked back into the main area. My goal was to find anyone who would listen, and I got louder and louder until a young officer walked over to silence me.

"I need to report an American who was just abducted," I said loudly. "The more time we waste, the more time they will have to hurt him."

"Please, Miss," he said, "come over to my desk. I will listen to your story."

CHAPTER 73

THE YOUNG OFFICER MUST have been fairly new to the force because he made sure everything I had to say was written on the correct form, and he made copies of all the evidence I brought with me. Quite the opposite happened in the station at Capri. I certainly preferred the latter because he showed empathy and concern for my situation. I was hopeful his superior would feel the same.

After I had completed my story, I watched as the young officer relayed a short version to a blond gentleman who looked like an American. My thought had barely come to the surface when he walked my way.

"Miss," he said (in perfect English), "I am very sorry to hear of your situation. I am on loan from the U.S. embassy in Rome. The local consular agency has limited services, and you just happened to catch me returning paperwork to this station tonight. I have been in Venice for the past few weeks, catching everyone up on their forms and legalities."

"Oh my gosh! Are you a resident of the United States?" I asked.

"Yes, I was born and raised in New York. My name is Lee."

"Super!" I exclaimed, "Hopefully you have influence and someone—anyone—can start looking for my good friend who has disappeared."

"Do you have both of your passports with you?" he questioned.

"Yes, I do. I also have a recent picture of him on my camera."

I reached into my bag to pull them out, and I handed them to Lee. As I did, Shiloh jumped off of my lap and started jumping up on his leg. I watched as he reached down, picked up the little guy, and started petting him.

"So," he said, "this is the puppy who created all of this fuss. Hopefully we can get everyone back together again soon."

The look on Lee's face—and the way he was caring for Shiloh—helped me relax, and I suddenly felt as though we were on the right path to finding Michael. Within a few short minutes, Lee had several officers alerted. They were heading to the Rialto Bridge.

"I hate to be negative," Lee said, "but I also think you and I should drive to the hospital to confirm he hasn't been taken there by someone. If we don't find him there, we'll zoom over to the bridge and retrace your steps."

"Thank you so much for taking the time to work with me on this," I said with a weak smile.

"Hey, I'd do it for anyone—but especially a pretty American," he said with a wink.

He walked closer to me and put both of his hands on my shoulders. It felt so good to feel someone giving 100 percent of their effort, and I said a silent prayer. I prayed the night would end on a positive note.

"My car is parked out back, so follow me. We'll get started tracking down your friend," he said, "The hospital isn't far from here."

Lee's pace was fast, and I had to almost run to keep up with him. My energy was slowly leaving my body, but I knew Michael would never rest if it were me left in that murky water. In no time, we were in his small car and moving much faster than the pace of traffic. I was surprised when Lee handed me an energy bar. It brought a smile to my face.

"Thanks," I said, opening the paper. "Guess you just can't beat that extra zip when you need it. Do you eat these a lot?"

"All the time," Lee said, "I got hooked in college and never gave them up."

Lee was right. It took only about 3 minutes to pull up in front of the hospital. "Leave the dog and follow me in," he said, exiting his door.

I felt like he had made the same trip before. His forcefulness seemed to get everyone at the main desk moving in the right direction, and I was surprised at his use of the Italian language. It only took two different displays of his embassy badge before we were standing in front of a young, female intern. I watched as the two of them spoke back and forth. Suddenly, both were looking directly at me. They seemed to be sizing me up to see whether I was strong enough to take their discussion in English.

"What?" I quizzed, looking back and forth into their eyes.

"This intern just told me a John Doe was brought into the morgue about an hour ago. She asked whether we wanted to attempt to identify him?"

The look on both of their faces brought chills to my arms, and I covered my fear by looking downward. *Please, God, give me the strength to do this.*

"Of course we want to see if the body is Michael's," I answered.

My quick reply gave Lee the opening he needed. He spoke softly in Italian to the intern, and then he grabbed my hand as we followed her down the narrow hallway. Not one of us spoke a word. Once inside the elevator, I let out a deep sigh. Lee's hand squeezed mine, and he continued facing forward. By the silence, I knew both of us were trying to prepare for the worst possible scenario.

Once the elevator opened, we had yet another ten yards to go before entering the refrigerated morgue. The cold stopped me in my tracks. I immediately let go of Lee's hand and backed out of the room. It never dawned on me that I couldn't go through with it. The reality of it all hit me at the same time the chill hit my nostrils. There was absolutely no way I could look at a dead body. There was no way I could hold it together if it was Michael.

It all seemed so surreal. Wasn't it just earlier that very day that the two of us were holding hands, laughing, and kissing? Wasn't he the one who had flown all the way to Italy to save me from the bad guys? I knew in my heart of hearts that Michael was *the* man for me. I had placed a wall up over my feelings the past few years, and he had torn it down piece by piece. Every look, every touch, every kiss warmed me to my very soul.

"I can't do this," I said as Lee walked out into the hallway to find me.

"Yes, you can," he answered. "It may take you a while, but you can do this."

"I need a few minutes alone," I said as I walked past Lee and down the long hallway.

I needed time—time to think, time to pray. I found a corner and pushed my back up against it. As I slid down to the floor, I reached into my purse to pull out my devotional. "I am beside you. Follow in all things My guiding. Marvels beyond all your imaginings are unfolding. Remember to Me a miracle is only a natural happening. A wonderful future is before you. A future of unlimited power. Just be a channel. Be used. Ask. Ask."

I immediately felt a great peace inside. I knew I could do what I had to do. I knew miracles happened daily, and I also knew I wasn't being pushed more than I could endure. I took another deep breath and got to my feet. I walked back toward Lee and the cold room that was called a morgue. *I can do this. I can ask to see the body.*

CHAPTER 74

ONCE AGAIN, LEE TOOK my hand and led the way. We went behind the young intern and into the refrigerated room. We stood still as she checked a clipboard to determine which drawer to open. She motioned with her hand for us to follow, and we fell in line behind her to the last row of closed chambers. She looked back to get confirmation I could perform the identification. I nodded and moved in closer—despite knowing she would pull out a lifeless body.

Gently, she pulled on the latch. As if in slow motion, she brought out a body covered with a sheet. As she pulled down the bright white sheath to expose his face, I took a deep breath and looked directly at the gurney. What I saw brought me to my knees.

"Oh dear God!" I exclaimed before vomiting on the floor.

"Carrie, are you all right?" questioned Lee.

The intern was soon holding my forehead, and Lee was grabbing every loose towel he could find to come to my rescue. I felt like the wind had been knocked out of me.

"Relax, sit back, and take a deep breath," the intern said over and over. Her gentle urging helped me regain my composure, and I leaned against one wall.

"I am so very sorry for your loss," she said while applying a damp towel to my face.

When I finally looked up, I could see Lee still standing over the body. I stood up, walked over to him, and looked directly at the body for a second time.

"Lee, this is *not* Michael," I said in a low voice. "I was so thankful it wasn't that I just lost it. It is, however, the gondolier who jumped on us and pulled a knife on Michael."

Lee's eyes widened, and I knew he was having a hard time digesting what had just happened. His eyes left mine and lowered back down to the body. He pulled even more of the sheath down and took out his phone. He snapped a quick picture, called the precinct, and ushered me out of the room.

"Thank God it wasn't your friend," he finally said, "You and I are now heading to the Rialto Bridge to try to find him—hopefully alive."

CHAPTER 75

Y<small>OU'D HAVE THOUGHT</small> I'<small>D</small> been gone for days by the way Shiloh greeted me when we got back into Lee's car. I was certain he knew something was wrong based on my demeanor. Animals seem to pick up on the smallest changes in behavior, and he had always been in tune with my mood swings. Of course, it didn't help that he had been taken away for a couple days from his comfort zone. It really felt good to hold his warm body close to me again.

We were soon flying in and out of traffic, and one look at Lee and the speedometer told me he had no problem with breaking any speed limits. I kept watching out the windows to look for the bridge where everything had gone wrong earlier. As I looked at my watch, I thought, *The sooner we get to the scene, the sooner we will find Michael.* Going over what just happened in my mind brought goose bumps to my arms. *Thank you, God, for getting me through that horrible ordeal.*

"This is the side of the bridge where you two waited for the gondola, right?" Lee asked.

"Yes, this is it. Park anywhere, and we can walk from here," I answered.

From the place where Lee stopped the car, I couldn't see any uniformed men. We had just spent an hour at the hospital, though, so perhaps they were under the bridge already. My curiosity was running rampant as we exited the car, and I quickly showed Lee the tree where we stood waiting for the gondola to arrive two hours before.

The scene was eerily the same as before. There was the dim lighting, the girl in the ticket booth, and one boat pulled next to the sidewalk. I could see by the name that it wasn't the same gondola we sat in. I immediately wondered whether the officers had already questioned the girl and suggested we walk over to talk to her.

Lee agreed, and as we made our way toward her booth, he used his his cell to check out the location of the officers directed to the bridge area earlier. For a split second, it seemed like déjà vu. There she was with earphones on, head bent down, reading a book. I actually felt as though I were reliving a dream sequence, and I tried to shake it off as we walked closer to her.

"The officers are telling me they interviewed her, but she saw nothing," he said.

"What?" I said, raising my voice, "Let's try it one more time."

"Miss, do you remember me?" I quizzed.

"*Si,* I do. You asked about ticket prices earlier," she answered.

"Do you remember when I returned and walked up to a gondolier by the name of Donato? He was right there with a young girl holding a dog in his boat," I said, pointing to where the other gondola was parked.

"We have no Donato working here," she answered.

Before I could say anything else, Lee broke in by showing her a picture on his cell phone. It was the body we just saw in the morgue. The minute she looked at it, her eyes got big, and her face showed fear. She attempted to turn away, but Lee's arm forced her head to look back at him.

"I can see by your expression that you know him," Lee said, "Who is he?"

"I cannot say any more," she said, looking down. " He will hurt me if I say more. Please do not ask me about this man."

"He cannot hurt you anymore," Lee said, "He is in the morgue at the hospital, and this is why we are trying to identify him."

Her face changed from scared to surprised. She showed true relief in her expression.

"He came to me yesterday and told me he needed to use one of the gondolas," she said. "I told him it was not possible, and he grabbed my wrist and turned it hard—very hard. He told me to make it happen or he would come back and knife up my face ... I think that is how you say it in English, no?"

"You mean he said he would disfigure your face?" I chimed in.

"That is what I mean," she said, eyes welling up with tears.

"You do not have to be afraid anymore," Lee said. "Did you notice anything different about him or anything that stood out?"

"He was very mean," she said. "I also noticed a tattoo on his wrist when he reached for my hand. It was a small Italian flag surrounded by fire."

"Oh my God!" I exclaimed. "That is the same tattoo all the men had back in Capri—the men trying to extort money. You definitely need to let the locals know about this, Lee."

"I'm on it," he retorted, and he turned his back as he started to dial on his cell.

I felt badly for the young girl we were staring at. I could only imagine her fright, and I was thankful she would not have any repercussions from that horrible man. One more thought did occur to me, though: "Do you remember the woman who was in the gondola holding the small dog?"

"*Si*," she said, nodding her head.

"Have you ever seen her before?" I asked.

"She works in a booth over in the Rialto market. I don't think she knew him though. She is very quiet, and I think the mean man found her only because she worked nearby."

Lee was now off his phone, and once again, he joined in on the conversation. I was able to catch him up, and he suggested we walk up and down the waterway to look for any clues as to where either of the two men would have pulled themselves up on the cement.

"The police are on the opposite side of the bridge, so let's you and I take this side," he said grabbing my hand. "With a little luck, we might find your friend."

CHAPTER 76

Thank goodness Lee had a flashlight in his car because my eyes never were good at night. I pointed to the approximate spot in the water where the two went overboard, and we worked our way down from there. I had grabbed one of Michael's sweatshirts before I left the hotel (thinking I might need it if the night cooled down). It occurred to me to let Shiloh smell it before I put him down—just in case he could smell the places Michael had been.

We walked and pushed leaves and sticks with our feet for quite a while. Every time one of us thought we noticed something on the walkway, we would either kick at the ground or bend down to check it out. It was hard for me to stop checking my watch every few minutes. I knew how important the timeline was in terms of finding any clues before tourists trampled over our paths once daylight dawned.

Nothing. Absolutely nothing. We mutually agreed to cross over the bridge so I could show him where I pulled the gondola over after the guys went into the water. The steps were too much for Shiloh, and I reached down to pick him up. As I did, my eyes caught a red smattering of something on the top step. I reached for the flashlight and cast a glow on the cobblestone.

"Do you think this is anything?" I asked.

"It could be if we find more of it," he answered.

We slowed our pace and followed the smattering across the bridge and down the steps to the other side. My heart started to race, and I wasn't sure what to expect as we continued walking next to the water. It did look like blood, but I certainly didn't want to get my hopes up. I was fairly positive Michael had been knifed before he entered the water, so there was a good chance he was still bleeding when he got out of the water.

Shiloh was starting to get fidgety in my arms, so I set him down and kept him close on his lead. His sense of smell was really good, and as we were walking and continuing to notice the crimson color every so often, he was pulling us forward at record pace. I knew his little nose could have the scent of any small varmint, so I didn't really pay much attention as he headed into the bushes at one point.

"Here, over here," Lee said, motioning me closer to the water's edge.

He was right. There was more than a smattering of red where his flashlight was pointing. It actually looked like blood. A lot of blood. You could see where something or someone had been dragged up past the waterline and onto the cobblestones. *How was it we were the first to find this? It couldn't have been more obvious.*

As Lee and I were assessing everything within the flashlight's glow, Shiloh seemed to be intrigued back in the heavy bushes. He kept pulling until he finally got my attention. I reached out and moved the light in Lee's hand past the cement. I focused on the end of the lead. Something was reflecting back at us. *What on earth?*

"There," I said, pointing. "What is that?"

Lee reached down and picked it up. He shrugged his shoulders and seemed to dismiss whatever it was. As he started to throw it back into the shrubs, I asked again.

"Just some old jack knife," he said.

"Wait a minute, I know that knife!" I exclaimed.

I reached for it and moved it under the light. As I shifted it around in my hand, I remembered Michael showing me the knife earlier. It was the very same pocket knife he had carried around since his dad had died. The only difference was that it had blood stains on it.

CHAPTER 77

BY THE TIME LEE called the officers over to the area, another thirty minutes had passed. More flashlights and more hands determined nothing else in the shrubs. One officer was quite adamant he had scoured the entire area, and I made a mental note of his badge number. I wasn't sure what it was about him, but my inner self told me he was either lying or just plain lazy. My concentration was interrupted as Lee took me aside.

"It's getting late, Carrie. Why don't you let me take you back to your hotel and allow the authorities to take over from here."

"I hate to give up," I answered, "but I know I'm really getting tired. I guess I'll let you drive me back. I'll try to rest a short while."

"Don't think of it as giving up," Lee said. "I promise you, I will do everything in my power to find your friend."

As we headed to the car, I couldn't help but look down for clues the entire way back. Shiloh's nose never left the cobblestones, and it didn't occur to me to lift him up again as we got to the steps of the bridge. It was at the top that he started pulling me over to the edge. We had been so focused on following the trail of blood, we had gotten tunnel vision. We had never widened our search. His persistence forced me to follow his lead. The dark shadows hid even his white fur from my eyes. I called his name a couple times before he emerged back into our light dragging a T-shirt in his mouth. A bloody T-shirt.

"Shiloh, what do you have, little guy?" I quizzed.

I knelt down and pulled the shirt out of his mouth. As I lifted it closer to the light, I noticed the orange Texas Longhorns emblem. It was definitely Michael's shirt—the one he was wearing as he fell into the murky water. As I held it up, a rip came into view. It was still wet … not only with water, but also with blood.

"Oh my God!" I exclaimed, "This does not make me feel any better, Lee."

"How did the uniforms miss finding this?" Lee quizzed.

"My thoughts exactly," I said. "I'm beginning to think we are the only two people who actually care about finding Michael alive."

We didn't have anything to place the shirt in, so I wrapped it in Michael's sweatshirt, and we hurriedly walked back to the car. We drove to the station, and Lee was able to find a clerk to log our evidence before he took me to my hotel. Even the energy bar handed to me wasn't going to help. Lee walked me to my room, and I was once again inside safe walls. Exhausted but safe, I placed a chair under the door handle to ensure my privacy.

"Good boy, Shiloh! We'd have never found Michael's shirt without you."

CHAPTER 78

I WASN'T SURE HOW long I had been in bed, but it seemed like I had tossed all night with very little sleep. I would never be able to forgive myself if something horrible happened to Michael as I slept. He was tough, but maybe not as tough as the gang members hoping for easy money.

I learned just how tough he was when I finally eased out of bed. The sun was coming in through the sheer drapes, and I was walking toward the bathroom for a warm shower when I glanced down. On the floor, under the door, I saw an envelope. Chills ran up my arms knowing those men were so close to me as I slept—close enough to leave yet another note.

I reached down and took it over to the bed with me. The envelope had no writing on the outside, and it wasn't sealed. I inhaled before I pulled out the folded piece of paper. *We have your boyfriend. $100,000 in American bills. Come at nine o'clock tonight, or he is a dead man. Come alone. Piazza San Marco. We will find you for the exchange.*

I picked up the room phone and called the police station. I asked for Lee. He answered immediately, and I read the note to him.

"I'll be there in thirty minutes to pick you up. I'll bring you something to eat," he said.

I was already in the lobby when Lee arrived. I had placed the note in one of my plastic cosmetic bags, and I handed it to him to read and hold for additional evidence.

"Tell me you think this is a good sign that Michael is alive," I said.

"I think it's a real good sign, or how could they expect to get the money?"

I watched as Lee read and reread the note. I had no clue what our next move would be, and I was anxious to hear his thoughts. After placing the note in his back pocket, he handed me a cappuccino and asked me to show him the way to the outside patio. Both of us were deep in thought when we finally sat down to have some of the pastries he had brought with him. It was too early for any waitstaff to be around, and we basically had the place to ourselves.

"I've got to show up tonight, you know," I finally said.

"I figured you'd say that. There are several problems, though, and I'm sure you realize what they are."

"I know I don't have a hundred grand," I said laughing.

"And I know Italy's Central Intelligence Agency, who I just called, won't let you show up alone in the market. You see, this is now their case because of the ransom and kidnapping," Lee said.

"Did we have to bring them into this?" I questioned.

"If you want the bad guys to be caught, money to carry, and Michael to be released, I would say yes," Lee answered, nodding his head in affirmation.

"Tell me I can still work with you?" I questioned.

"Yes, because you are an American and I am with the American embassy, they have allowed me on the case."

"Good," I said, patting his hand, "What's next?"

"We need to meet with them in fifteen minutes (back at the station). There, we'll devise a plan. The more time elapsed, the higher chance of foul play."

I opted to leave Shiloh in the room for the next outing, and we finished our breakfast and walked to Lee's car. I was starting to feel in control once again—and certainly fortunate to find such a willing and accommodating individual working for the local embassy. My mind was having a hard time figuring out how everything would go down, but I was more than willing to be involved in any plot to speed Michael's release.

Once at the station, Lee led the way to a back office decorated only with a round table and several chairs. Two men in suits stood and introduced themselves as we entered. I could see by the files and box in front of them that they had pictures and evidence submitted locally and at the Capri police station. Lee pulled out the latest note and placed it before them. Both men read it and looked directly at me.

"We want you to know that these people are members of a gang we have been trying to put away for the past two years. We are truly astonished you have been dealing with their members as long as you have without being hurt. You have done as much—if not more—than any one undercover agent in our employ."

As the one agent was talking, the other was placing pictures in front of me for identification (I assumed). I looked down and immediately spotted three of the seven individuals with whom I had come in contact over the past month.

"It is our hope you can identify one or more of these gang members—and that we can mutually work together to put a stop to their unconventional tactics," the first agent stated. "Do you recognize any of these men?"

"These three right here," I said, pushing their pictures toward the agents.

"Excellent," the first agent said. "Speaking candidly, we believe one or more of these gang members will be involved in the transaction this evening. Under normal circumstances, we would bring in a female agent to handle it tonight. However, they specifically asked for you, and they know who you are. We would like to ask you to consider putting on a hidden microphone and making the exchange tonight. Of course, we will have undercover agents nearby for your protection. There is, as in everything, some risk involved."

"Are you are telling me there's a high percentage chance you can catch these horrible gang members *and* get Michael back safely tonight with my help?" I asked.

"Yes, that's exactly what we are saying," the agent said. "We realize this is a big decision on your part, so if you would like us to leave the room and let you think about it, we will understand."

"I don't have to think about it," I replied, "I want them caught, and I want my friend back. I'm willing to do whatever it takes to make it happen."

CHAPTER 79

I GUESS MY ANSWER told them everything they needed to know because, within minutes, we were all brainstorming and trying to formulate a fairly elaborate plan. It made me feel good to know we were all working toward one goal, which was stopping those horrible men from preying on innocent people. *Hang in there, Michael, we're coming to your rescue!*

The room soon filled up with more and more men—some in suits, some in uniforms. Each man was told where he would be standing, what he would be wearing, and what specific activity he would be undertaking.

I was told the money would be the last thing to arrive because they were requisitioning it from their main branch. A female agent entered the room and requested that I follow her to have a hidden microphone placed on my body. She was very professional. By the time she was finished, I felt like my entire upper body was taped in place. She suggested I remain taped with sound off until the meeting.

Once I was walked back to the initial room, the sound on the microphone was tested and retested. All the levels were adjusted. Navy blue ball caps were brought in and given to everyone. Each cap had a New York Yankees logo on it, and they would be very easy to spot. I was told over and over that if I felt like I was in danger, I should make a specific sign to abort the mission.

The main agent seemed very traditional, and he did things by the book; hence, we were told we would rehearse the mission in the piazza in an hour. All of us would be driven over in an unmarked van. I was given a shopping bag with newspapers in it as a substitute for the money. Everyone was told to adjust their watches to a specific time. Introductions were made to ensure face verification. It was definitely the real deal.

CHAPTER 80

F OR LACK OF A better word, the *practice* went off without a hitch. I felt
very secure, and I was able to spot each and every ball cap in the piazza.
I certainly wasn't so naive as to think it would be so easy once the tourists
and locals started gathering, but at least it helped the odds. The microphone
seemed to be working well, and my suggestion to use an earpiece allowed
contact and direction.

One hour after we returned to the main branch, Lee drove me back to
the hotel. It was suggested by the authorities that Lee remain with me for the
day. A plain-clothes officer was designated to remain inside the hotel lobby.
Cell phone numbers were exchanged, and they were predicting an uneventful
afternoon.

Shiloh greeted us at the hotel room door, and both Lee and I headed
to the sofa to relax, put our feet up, and take in everything that had just
transpired.

"Did they really say actual money was being requisitioned for me to take
to the piazza tonight?" I asked.

"I wondered when that fact would soak in," Lee answered.

"Good grief! I suppose I'll have to sign over my first born in the event
that it's actually taken from me," I said, starting to chuckle. "They must do
this sort of thing enough to know it might be lost, right?"

"One would assume," he answered.

I walked over to open a window and asked whether Lee wanted me to
order room service or go down to the restaurant for something to eat. We
decided on room service, and I reached into my vest to get some cash. My
hand felt something other than paper bills, and I pulled out Michael's cell
phone. He must have put it in my vest pocket for safe keeping when we headed
to the gondola for the initial exchange to get Shiloh back.

As I went to place it on the table, I felt it vibrate. I looked at the screen.
And then it hit me. Michael must have found a cell phone and sent me a

text. *Over r heads. Get help.* The message arrived three hours prior. At least I knew he was alive. And I was certain he would be thankful I brought in the reinforcements.

After Lee read the text, he contacted the station and relayed the message to the lead agent on our case. They asked that we take the cell phone down to the special agent in the lobby so he could place it in the proper hands. I was standing and still hyper, so I grabbed the phone and told Lee I'd run it down the stairs to the agent.

I hadn't been out the door and down the hallway more than half a minute before I had a strange feeling. It was the same feeling I had a few years prior when I felt someone watching me as I washed my car in the back alley of my apartment complex. Back then, I looked around and spotted a man on a rooftop looking down at me with binoculars. There was no rooftop here, only a narrow hallway in a major hotel. *My mind must be playing tricks on me,* I thought. I proceeded down the stairs to the lobby.

After handing the phone to the agent, I opted not to mention my concern regarding the strange feeling I just had. I did, however, start looking more closely in the hallway before I put the key into my door again. I found myself rationalizing as I walked back and forth—after all, they had been to my very door several times. *How would they know I was in rather than out? How would they know I wouldn't come back and catch them in the act?*

It made perfect sense to me. *Why wouldn't they have a room in the same hotel to be able to watch my movements?* There were doors on both sides of the room. It could be possible they were occupying one of those rooms. All three doors looked the same. The only exception was a thin cord coming out of the top trim on one of the doors. My eyes traced it over several more doors and directly to the back of the hotel security camera at the end of the hallway. *Now why would that cord be going into a hole above the adjoining door to my room? There actually shouldn't be any cord coming out of that camera. It should be self-contained with a simple video tape.*

The chills came back to my arms. Maybe I had that eerie feeling because someone *was* actually watching me. I attempted to act nonchalant, and I opened the door to my room. Lee was still on the sofa, and he asked whether everything went as planned.

176

"I handed the cell over, but I came up with a new theory of my own," I said as I walked toward him.

I told him exactly what I had found in the hallway—and my thoughts on how they might have bugged the security camera. Lee's head began to nod in agreement, and I could see he thought it very possible. He wanted to relay the thought to the agent in the lobby. He opted to call the agent's cell, and he told him about the additional cord going into the room next door. I heard him suggest checking the hotel register to see who was assigned to the adjoining room.

A short five minutes later, we heard the sound of multiple voices in the hallway. We walked to our closed door and placed our ears up next to it. I could immediately identify one voice as the agent in the lobby and another as the maid who worked so hard at cleaning the blood off our door. He must have found her in the hallway doing her routine room cleaning. Both Lee and I nodded in agreement; we decided to open the door and check it out.

In the short time it took us, the maid had already unlocked the neighboring door and left it wide open. I noticed the *do not disturb* sign on the doorknob. We stood outside looking in, and we couldn't believe what we saw. The agent had pulled a blanket from under the bed. He opened it up to reveal a hand gun, several bags of some white substance, and a brown envelope containing a whole lot of American bills. A round table in the room had a monitor set up with a full view of the outside hallway. No one would simply leave all of that behind. Someone was definitely coming back.

CHAPTER 81

W E WERE IMMEDIATELY TOLD not to enter and to go back into our own room until we heard what was going on. I couldn't help but smile thinking how pleased both Dr. Gabel and Michael would be when they learned how clever I had been. Even Lee gave me a high five as we entered our room.

"Don't get too excited, Nancy Drew!" Lee said, "You still need to orchestrate a smooth transaction tonight to get your friend back."

"Hey, if anyone can do it tonight, I can," I said.

My adrenaline was starting to charge, and there was absolutely no way I could nap after finding the hidden camera next door. I didn't want to risk leaving the room, so I suggested we play some cards to make the time go by faster. My mother had taught me more than enough games, and solitaire was definitely not an option.

The afternoon dragged by, and it was hard not to think about what would happen when the person or persons came back to the adjoining room. The authorities couldn't simply make an arrest because doing so could upset all our plans for getting Michael back and capturing one or more of the gang members. My thoughts were confirmed when Lee was contacted and told that everything had been placed as it had been found. They said they would only monitor the situation until the money was handed off in the piazza.

The authorities decided to station an agent in the hallway. He would be wearing maintenance overalls and painting the walls as his cover. This would ensure protection for both Lee and me. It definitely eased my mind knowing no confrontation would be taking place. We were told to leave our room well in advance of anyone returning. We were advised to take everything with us because they would be moving us to a safe house, and we would not be returning to the hotel.

They didn't need to tell us twice. Within ten minutes Lee was carrying my suitcase, and I had Shiloh in my arms. As we opened our door, we immediately noticed the undercover agent painting. His simple nod was all the assurance we needed to proceed down the stairway. We were told they would check us out of the hotel so we could proceed to the front door. They told us to look for a black sedan as we exited. A dark BMW was directly in front, and the time spent commuting to the safe house was less than a half hour.

"Whew," I said as we pulled up in front of a small home on a hillside. "I'm glad we got in and out without our hotel neighbor returning."

"You can say that again," Lee answered, "Let's head into this house and make it our own for the next hour or so."

The driver opened the front door for us and told us to keep it locked. He said we should keep the draperies closed and wait for a phone call. We did just as he advised.

CHAPTER 82

B Y THE TIME THE phone rang, I was more than willing to get reconnected again with Michael. Shiloh had found a nesting spot on the bed, and I had made sure—for the tenth time—that the tape was secured to my skin. Lee was sitting at a desk doing some paperwork, and both of us jumped when we heard his cell go off.

"The time has finally arrived," Lee said, disconnecting from the caller.

"Thank goodness," I answered and walked over to get my sweater.

I didn't really feel nervous; I felt ready to get everything behind me. *Dear God, please protect all involved tonight and return Michael safely from the men holding him.*

The next several minutes were a blur. We were picked up and carted to the station, and I was taken immediately to have my wires checked for sound. I was given a heavy, cloth shopping bag with the money, and I was told to hand it over freely since they had an electronic tracer buried inside one of the packs of bills. All the agents who were going to be in the piazza were brought into the room, and I was introduced a second time to them … this time with their hats on. Michael's picture was distributed to all for instant identification.

I was told that, after the exchange took place, I should walk Michael into the church. Men would be waiting to direct us to safety. I was given a bright red jacket to wear, which would make it easy for all the agents to follow me. If, for any reason, they would not relinquish Michael, I was told to raise both hands in the air for immediate help.

We were soon ushered into a van and taken to an area on the backside of St. Mark's square before being let out. I was told to stay as close to the front of the church as possible. The piazza was quite expansive, and continued communication was a necessity for adequate protection.

"I see the perfect table, and I am walking toward it now," I said, hands up to cover my lips. "There are several women knitting and showing their handmade quilts, so I'm fairly certain they aren't part of any gang."

"Copy that," I heard in my ear.

I was surprised at how heavy the money was—and even more surprised at how many people were still in the piazza at such a late hour. Once I sat down and placed the bag under my legs, I started to look around. I knew there were at least eight ball caps out there, and I focused on finding New York Yankee logos.

My eyes soon found one man, who was picking up trash with a long litter stick. Another man wearing the cap was reading an Italian newspaper only three tables away. Yet another was graciously opening St. Mark's door for tourists. It was as if I were solving a puzzle of *Where's Waldo*, and my eyes were able to find him everywhere.

My concentration was broken by a pigeon landing in front of me and eating a cracker someone had dropped. Watching the bird was a great deterrent from looking around, and I was able to smile and relax a little as the pigeon played with his find before eating it.

I had only been seated about ten minutes before I heard talk in my earpiece.

"Believe subject to be walking your way from far side of piazza. Accompanied by taller gentleman wearing green. Please locate and confirm."

My eyes started scanning from left to right. Just how far was *the far side of piazza*? I could see no one wearing green.

"Cannot visualize," I responded, feeling dumb.

"Doors at St. Mark's are at twelve o'clock. Subject is at three o'clock. Please locate and confirm."

Once again, my eyes started scanning the crowd. I was looking in one particular quadrant and saw the man in green. I started watching them as they walked my way, and I looked for anything to confirm it was Michael. *Please let this be Michael.* The sun was going down directly in my eyes, and I was squinting with my hand over my forehead to get a visual.

"Subject is not—repeat, not—Michael," I finally said into the microphone.

"Copy that."

If they wanted their money, why weren't they on time? I wondered. I glanced down at my watch and saw I had only been sitting for ten minutes. I couldn't let the thought creep into my mind that they wouldn't come after their money.

They just had to come. We had worked so hard to ensure my safety—it never occurred to me that they would stand me up. I took a deep breath and started looking around the piazza once again.

My eyes were scanning each and every man walking when I decided to check out anyone already seated at a table. There were so many tables, but just after I began my scan, I saw him! *Could it actually be Michael?* He was seated with two other men and looking down. I watched for any movement that would confirm it was him. As his head raised, his eyes locked onto mine, and I knew beyond any doubt that it was Michael. *Thank you, God.*

"I have found subject. Wearing bright blue and sitting with two other men at nine o'clock," I said.

"Copy that. Hold position until we can confirm."

It seemed like an eternity before they came back into my earpiece with their confirmation.

"Continue to hold your position. We have a fix on subject."

Time passed: five minutes, ten minutes, fifteen minutes. *What on earth are they waiting for?* Michael did not look up again, and I was ready to scream. About the time I was going to break the silence, the three of them stood up. They were walking my way. Michael was in between both men, and our eyes were once again locked on each other. I heard talking in my earpiece.

"Proceed with exchange when subject reaches you."

Closer and closer they came, and my heart started to pound faster and faster. I decided to continue sitting with the heel of my sandal resting on the bag of money under the table. All I wanted was to make sure they would release Michael and no one would be hurt.

All of a sudden, they stood before me. One of the men had his hand in his pocket, and I could see the butt of a gun peeking out. Their heads were looking around, and nothing was said for at least a minute as they verified I was alone.

"Please don't harm me with your gun," I said, giving the agents a heads-up.

"Do you have our money?"

"Yes," I answered, "it is here under the table."

"Show it to us," one of the men ordered.

I reached down and slid the bag out in full sight of the men. I slowly opened the zipper and exposed the money. I looked up about the time one of them reached into the bag to confirm there were American bills all the way to the bottom. I saw his sadistic smile as he reached down to lift the satchel. The other man pushed Michael down on a chair next to me.

"Do not follow us. Do not involve yourself with us again."

The men turned and started walking away from our table. My earpiece started making noise again.

"Both of you stand up and walk into the church. Do not turn around."

I grabbed Michael's hand, guided him up, and told him to walk into the church with me. I could tell he wasn't standing straight and favoring his right side. As I looked down, I could see some blood oozing out from under the shirt he had been given to wear. He noticed my stare and took my chin in his hand.

"I'm all right, Carrie," he whispered, "It's only superficial. I just need another bandage."

"Thank God," I answered.

The very minute we entered the church, we were met by agents who escorted us to a side door, into a black van, and safely down the streets of Venice.

CHAPTER 83

BEFORE THE VAN HAD rounded the first corner, Michael pulled me into his arms. After what seemed like forever, he gently took my face and directed my lips to his lips. What I thought was going to be a welcome home kiss ended up being much, much more. I could feel the raw emotion exploding as our lips pushed against each other. Time stood still. When his lips finally left mine, he continued kissing my eyes, ears, and neck. Chills ran down my entire being.

It was as though we couldn't get close enough. He kept pulling my body closer and closer until, finally, the trance was broken by the driver coming to a complete stop in front of the station.

"To be continued," Michael said, helping me out of the van.

"Promises, promises," I answered as I smiled.

We were shown to the back room where Michael was given immediate attention by a paramedic, and I was directed out an adjoining door to have the microphone disconnected. The female agent worked quickly, and I didn't mind the tug of the tape knowing it was off for good. By the time I walked back into the room, several agents were questioning Michael. I sat there listening to his ordeal of the past few days. As I watched his mannerisms, I couldn't help but think how hard I was falling for him. Absence really did make the heart grow fonder.

CHAPTER 84

WE WERE EVENTUALLY TOLD we could occupy the safe house for the night, and then we would be picked up in the morning for transport to a small airport where we could fly directly into Naples. I questioned whether they were able to apprehend any of the gang members or the money, and their only comment was, "Everything worked out well." I could do without the pat on the back knowing Michael was back safely.

You'd have thought Shiloh was reunited with his best friend when we first walked into the house. It actually was a surprise for me to see him bound toward Michael's arms first, and I had to chuckle as I watched them bond. Eventually, the three of us got together for a group hug, and it didn't take long before his little heart stopped beating so fast. As we pulled away, I looked at Michael with a serious look.

"You know," I said, "I really was worried about you."

"And you think I wasn't worried about you?" he questioned as he took me into his arms.

"I'll admit it, you have grown on me," I said with a smile.

"Good, because I think we owe it to one another to express some of our feelings tonight," Michael answered.

The hour was late, and it didn't take much to convince us to hold each other and admit some of our innermost thoughts to one another. Michael reached over to flip on the radio, and Dean Martin was singing "Volare." He reached for my hand and pulled me close. Out of the blue, he started swaying back and forth—we were moving to the music.

"All I thought about was you alone in Venice … and me not being able to come to your rescue," he said.

"I knew you would if you could," I answered.

"That's just it," he said, "I wasn't sure you knew. I've had a wall up around my heart since it was broken three years ago. These feelings haven't been around lately, and I didn't want to blow it if you didn't have the same feelings."

"And," I cut in, "I didn't want to think of you more than a friend and neighbor, so I've been holding my guard up as well."

"Are you telling me we might have something here?" he quizzed.

"That's what I'm telling you."

Michael held me tighter and tighter as we moved to the music. Our bodies seemed as one, and as I reached up to kiss him, his lips met mine. Never before had I felt so secure, so safe. I didn't want the music to end. When it did, we both slid to the floor and fell asleep in each other's arms.

CHAPTER 85

I AWOKE TO SHILOH'S low whine. Morning had come, and I wasn't sure what time we would be picked up for the airport. I nudged Michael as I stood up, and I told him I was taking the dog for a quick walk.

"See if there's any coffee in the kitchen," I yelled, heading out the front door.

What a glorious morning it was. Even Shiloh seemed to sense we were on the tail end of our trip to Italy. His pace was back to prancing rather than pulling, and I had to laugh knowing how intuitive he had always been. We took a quick trip around the block, and as I entered the door, I smelled coffee brewing.

"You found some. Great!" I yelled.

I knew from the sound of the shower that Michael didn't hear my shout. I proceeded into the kitchen, poured a cup of coffee, and started checking the cupboards for any dry creamer. I spotted some on the top shelf. When I reached up to grab it, Michael surprised me by kissing my neck from behind.

"Good morning, beautiful," he said, turning me around. "For someone with no makeup on, you sure look good!"

"I bet you say that to all the girls," I replied with a smile. "Say, here's a question I never thought I'd be asking: how did you sleep?"

"Considering we fell asleep on the floor—and considering we had just been involved in a detailed rescue operation—I'd say I slept like a baby! Knowing you were in my arms made it all so worth it. What about you?"

"I, too, slept like a baby—thank you very much," I answered, smiling.

And, once again, he just looked at me. Those eyes. Those Brad Pitt eyes. They made me melt. I could see so much more depth in them than I could before he flew to join me in Italy. I would have absolutely no problem cuddling and staring into those eyes all day long. I was just about to tell him that very thought when his cell went off. He was on it for less than ten seconds.

"They'll be here in thirty minutes," he said, pulling me in close.

"Perfect timing for me to grab a shower," I said. "And just so you know, I'd much rather stay in your arms than be showering alone."

"Is that an invitation?" he asked with a smirk.

"No, just a thought to hold for future encounters."

CHAPTER 86

Fᴿᴏᴍ ᴛʜᴇ ᴛɪᴍᴇ ᴛʜᴇ agent picked us up to the time we boarded the plane, only a few hours had passed. Since I had first greeted Michael at the mission in Capri, he had always reached for my hand, but just lately, he was doing it more and more. It was a simple act, but one which I thoroughly enjoyed. Being kidnapped had made quite an impact on both of us, and we knew—more than anyone—how special our time was together.

You could tell we were anxious to land in Naples and find our way back to Capri. Both of us were talking about reuniting with Angelo and trying to imagine what he would say when we told him about the authorities apprehending the gang members responsible for causing so much havoc. I was already picturing in my mind how jubilant Sister Mary B. would be once she learned the children were safe and could enjoy going outside again. The two of us were more than ready to head back to the States, to the calmness of day-to-day living.

The flight went smoothly and was only half-full. This allowed me to hold and cuddle Shiloh, which seemed to relax both of us. By the time we touched land, we had decided on taking the hydrofoil to Capri. It was fun, and it got us to the mission quickly. We grabbed a taxi from there, and we were on our way.

CHAPTER 87

No amount of talking could have prepared us for the reception we received at the mission. The closest thing might be the Cinco de Mayo celebration in San Antonio every year. It was obvious the local authorities had already told both Sister Mary B. and Angelo because, as we turned down the old cobblestone path toward the mission, we could see a huge banner hanging on the bell tower. *Our heroes!* We both felt humbled ... and not much like heroes.

All the children were standing outside, holding posters with their handprints and names on them. The words *thank you* were printed everywhere. All the nuns and Angelo had small American flags, and they were waving them back and forth as we approached. Sister Mary B. had a big smile on her face, and as we got closer, she turned and started the children singing a familiar song: "If You're Happy and You Know It, Clap Your Hands."

So much joy was being transmitted from the small group of children and nuns. I felt as though I should hug each and every one—and that's exactly what Michael and I started doing, spontaneously. By the time we got to Sister Mary B., I could see a tear gently falling down her cheek. Angelo and his siblings ran over to both of us, and they were jumping up and down.

"I don't know how you did it, but I feel as though the weight of the world is off my shoulders," he said.

"You wouldn't believe everything that has happened," I said, "but the end result is that good prevailed over evil."

The children finished one song and went right into another song. All of us were swaying to the music, and Michael was lifting each child up onto his shoulders and zigzagging in between everyone. Our smiles never diminished for over an hour, and even Shiloh felt the excitement and was passed around from child to child. *Thank you, God, for this glorious outcome.*

CHAPTER 88

Sister Mary B. had a huge meal set up inside for all of us, and after enjoying her homemade pasta, we all started to wind down. Every so often, I would think about what Dr. Gabel had told me during our last phone call days before. He said I had one last mission. It was hard to believe I could do much more in Italy. I was hopeful he would see my research on Angelo was factual and that I had followed all of his instructions. Surely, he would help Angelo provide for his siblings.

There was so much for me to talk to Sister and Angelo about, and the three of us met in the library after everyone had gotten back to business as usual. It took me a few hours to go over my real identity and all I had been given to confirm Angelo's background. I shared how an unnamed benefactor wanted me to confirm that his role in life was to help the children at the mission. I told him how the individual wanted to bestow a gift for his act of kindness. I watched as Angelo sat in disbelief; his eyes clouded over with tears. I saw how Sister Mary B. comforted him and thanked God for everyone involved in his life.

Before I could tell Angelo how special he was, Michael came into the room with his phone. He handed it to me, and I knew who it had to be. I excused myself and headed for the hallway where I could be alone.

"Hello," I said.

"Hello, Carrie," Dr. Gabel replied, "I can now confirm the authorities are in control and have all the pertinent gang members arrested." His voice sounded even more feeble than it had during our phone conversation earlier, and it brought reality back quickly.

"Thank God," I said, "What else can I do for you?"

"Carrie, the reason I hired someone of your character is because I needed not only your discretion, but also your exuberance for life. I am well past having much joyful enthusiasm, but what I lack in fervor, I can and will supply in monetary subsidies. In the back of the portfolio you will find a sealed envelope. It should be handed to Angelo with just the two of you present."

"Of course," I said. "I will be happy to do this last act for you."

"I must commend you, Carrie, for far surpassing your duties as my liaison. You have acted with integrity, and I am most proud to have you in my employ. Now then, finish up in Italy and head back to the States. I will be in contact with you once you are home."

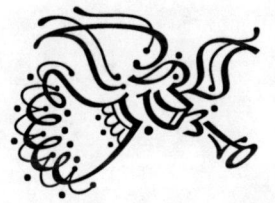

Part Three

CHARITY

CHAPTER 89

I HAVE TO ADMIT that my curiosity was piqued by the envelope I held in my hand. Because it was up to me to hand it over to Angelo, I thought long and hard about the place to present it to him. A smile came over my face when it occurred to me. The most appropriate place would be inside the church—the church that had provided a safety net for all the children for many years.

"Angelo, please sit with me in this front pew," I said, motioning with my hands.

"What is this about?" Angelo questioned.

"It is about honoring someone for their kindness. You did not question why your life turned out the way it did; instead, you simply acted. Someone in this wide world of ours would like to thank you for being you."

I placed the crisp, white envelope in Angelo's hand. He took it with the anticipation of a child opening a birthday present for the first time. Suddenly, he stopped halfway. He looked into my eyes, and I nodded for him to continue. He completed the tear and pulled out a check. His eyes widened and clouded over.

"Oh my God!" he said, "This is so much money. My prayers have been answered. Now I can build a decent orphanage for many, many children. I do not know what to say."

His arms felt warm as he hugged me, and his words were sincere as he said, "Thank you, thank you."

"You need not thank me for this gift," I said, "I am merely this benefactor's extended arms. I am only the one he was seeking to present this to you. You created this joy by your unselfish acts of human courage and morality."

CHAPTER 90

A NGELO COULD NOT WAIT to share the latest happenings with Sister Mary B., and we soon found ourselves gathered around the kitchen table. I found Michael in the gloomy hallway, and I asked him to follow me for a brainstorming session. As Angelo was relaying his new inheritance to all, he pulled out paper and a pen in an attempt to show what his thoughts were for a new orphanage.

"I envision a bright, open structure with a courtyard in the middle," he said. "In the center of the courtyard, I can picture a fountain with water flowing. The handprints of all the children who have and will take refuge there will surround the fountain in mortar. I can see colorful flowers, vines, and many, many fruit trees. No longer will the children and nuns be forced to conduct classes underground. Air and sunshine will be their school."

"Oh, Angelo," Sister Mary B. said, "it sounds so wonderful. You are a gift from God."

"No, Sister, my unknown benefactor and these two Americans are the angels from God," Angelo answered.

"It was our pleasure to help in any way we could. We totally believe in just causes, and so does your unknown guardian angel in the States," I said. "Unfortunately, we need to leave you to return home, but I would like to give you my address so you can update me on the progress of your upcoming project."

We all hugged and cried and walked out the door of the mission. We felt like we were walking on clouds. I attempted to give a hurried tour as Michael and I walked the piazza and entered the tram that descended the cliffs overlooking the Mediterranean. The gentle breeze and sunshine gave us the warmth of the Isle of Capri, and somehow we knew that a return trip was in our future.

By the time we took the hydrofoil back to Naples, gathered my things from the hotel, and settled into Michael's car rental, time was starting to take a toll on both of us. We shared driving the small car and opened all the windows as if we could take all the beauty of Italy back with us to the United States.

"Once we get to my B and B in Rome, let's make plane reservations for tomorrow. There is still one thing I'd like to take you to see and do before we leave Italy," I said.

"You mean, I actually get to see something else in Rome besides the small garden outside your bungalow's window?" he asked laughing.

CHAPTER 91

As darkness started to fall, we pulled into Rome. The lights of the city were breathtaking. *Thank you, God, for giving us just one more night before we leave this remarkable city.* It almost seemed like home when we entered the small bungalow. I walked over to open the window overlooking the flowered garden and placed Shiloh on the window sill.

"Dibs for taking a shower first," I said, heading into the bathroom.

"Okay. Shiloh and I will take in the night air and wait for you."

Nothing—and I mean *nothing*—seemed better than the hot water from that shower. As I stood there with my face next to the showerhead, it seemed as though the past few weeks were playing over and over again in my mind. I knew I was strong, but I also knew I was given the extra strength to persevere by a higher power watching over me.

"It's all yours," I said, walking out with my cozy robe on. "What I have to show you won't take very long, but it's so worth it."

Michael was in and out of the shower in record time, and we soon found ourselves walking hand in hand in the warm night air. I tried my best to point out some of the sights Angelo had shown me, and we soon found ourselves in front of the one thing I most wanted to share.

"There it is," I said with a sigh, "The Trevi Fountain. It dates back to 1762, when Bernini came up with the idea and Nicolo Salvi brought it to life."

I pulled two coins out of my vest and handed one to Michael.

"The saying goes that if we toss a coin into the fountain, we will return to Rome," I said, holding onto Michael's other hand.

"Then that is what we will do," he said. "On my count of three—one, two, three!"

The two of us tossed our coins up, and we watched as they came to rest under the water. As if in a movie, we turned to each other and kissed. It seemed to seal our resolve to return one day.

CHAPTER 92

MANDIE GREETED US AT the airport, and Missy seemed to tell us all off for the first hour after we walked into my apartment. As I looked around at my furnishings, I found a renewal in my own life. I was truly blessed to have such a nice place to live, such wonderful friends, and such a giving and heartwarming new employer.

I headed into the kitchen and came out with a bottle of wine.

"I propose a toast," I exclaimed as I handed them each a glass. "To good friends, the higher power watching over us, the small acts of kindness found around the world, and the freedom to reward their efforts."

It was appropriate that I was ending my first liaison job with my overhead light flickering. "Rejoice in the spring-time of the year. Let there be spring-time in your hearts. The full time of fruit is not yet but there is the promise of the blossom. Know surely your lives too are full of glad promise. Such blessings are to be yours. All is indeed well. Live in My sunshine and My love."

CHAPTER 93

THE CALENDAR AND BEAUTY of the neighborhood mums were telltale signs we were entering into the last few months of the year, but true seasons in Texas weren't always dictated by the simple turning of a page on my desktop. The one obvious sign time had passed since my European adventure was parked in front of my apartment complex. The white pearl hybrid with darkened windows was directly in my vision when I opened my blinds each morning, but accepting the fact that I was the owner still seemed like a dream. Anytime I got a feeling of superiority, though, my eyes automatically shifted to my mother's old, reliable Cutlass parked next to it. After seeing it, I would immediately become grounded again.

I was certain I would never forget the feeling I had as I held the envelope delivered by special courier a week after I unpacked. Even Shiloh couldn't figure out why I was still standing next to the door long after the van pulled away. Thinking back, I wasn't afraid to open it. My mind just kept flashing back to all the feelings I had over the past few months: confident, insecure, hopeful, suspicious. I had been on a roller coaster ride, and the bar holding me tight so I wouldn't fall out had been Michael.

I knew almost immediately what I needed to do before opening the envelope. I reached for my phone, dialed, and was just about to leave a message when he answered.

"Hey, been wondering when I'd hear from you," Michael said. "What's up?"

"Guess what I'm holding in my hand?" I asked with a giggle in my voice.

"No clue," he answered.

"Okay, I'll give you a hint," I said. "The return address is from Lawndale."

"I'll be there in fifteen minutes!" he said, hardly trying to hide his enthusiasm.

CHAPTER 94

I NEVER GAVE IT a thought that Shiloh always knew Michael was dropping by. I just chalked it up to a dog thing. But as he danced at my feet, it suddenly came to me: he could tell by my mannerisms and voice inflection. Smart dog. I picked him up and told him he had to wait just a short while for his buddy to arrive.

By the time I had made the popcorn and poured us some root beer, I heard his footsteps approaching my front door. I reached the knob and opened it just as he was about to knock.

"Are you ready to find out if all of our perils were worth it?" I jokingly asked.

"Did I not make it here in record time?" he said. "Of course I'm ready!"

Before I could turn to grab the bowl of popcorn, he reached out with both hands to hold my shoulders. His kiss on my forehead was soft—too soft. I arched my feet and reached up to place my lips on his. Ever since Italy, my feelings had accelerated, and I needed him to know—really know—how much he meant to me.

"Okay, you take the glasses, I'll grab the bowl, and we can have a seat on the couch," I said.

"Can you delay this any more?" he quizzed, smile on his face.

He was right. I wasn't eager to rush the envelope opening. I actually didn't want to rush anything ever again. Time could stand still if it wanted to. My adrenaline had been supercharged the entire time I was out of the country, and winding down to a snail's pace was something I had started to value more and more.

"Have you driven the white beauty yet?" he asked, putting a kernel into his mouth.

"Can't make myself do it until I know if I can afford to pay the insurance," I said laughing.

"What happened to the positive attitude?" he asked.

"Nothing happened to it—I'm just cautiously optimistic."

As I picked up the unopened envelope, Michael started a drum roll with his fingers on the cushion. Once he noticed I was still doing nothing, he reached into his pocket and pulled out his knife so I could open the sealed document. The sight of it brought memories flooding back. There it was: the same knife I had found with blood all over it next to the water's edge in Venice. My heart fell yet again as I remembered the fear I had not knowing whether he was alive or dead. Michael sensed my anxiety.

"Hey, Carrie, it's all right. Everything turned out okay." His left arm pulled me closer as if he were cuddling a small child. "Stop torturing yourself by reliving the past. This should be one of the happiest days of your life."

He was right, logically speaking. But I couldn't help but wonder how one turned off the feeling of sudden emptiness experienced by not knowing everything would turn out all right. Hopefully Michael would never know that feeling.

I sliced open the envelope and unfolded one page of white stationary. As I did, two checks fell onto my lap. We ignored them until we could read the letter. From the opening sentence, our eyes were glued to the page. *Did he really feel that way? Had he truly researched everything we did in each and every city throughout Italy? Was it actually possible to receive reports back so soon from the authorities in Italy?* Three paragraphs, and still no mention of further employment or the amount on the checks that had fallen face down. *When on earth would Dr. Gabel get to the point?* By the fourth paragraph, he did.

"Finished reading?" I asked.

"Yeah, I'm finished. Want to read it over again?" he questioned.

I looked into his eyes and immediately saw that he was kidding. Together, we picked up the checks and turned them over. If, in fact, time could have stood still, it would have been perfect for it to do so at that moment.

"Pinch me," I said while leaning over to kiss Michael.

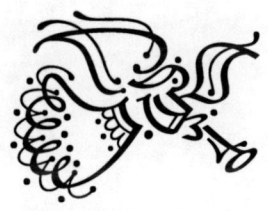

Epilogue

ONE YEAR LATER

CHAPTER 95

STAYING BUSY WASN'T HARD for me because a great deal of my time was taken up with research for Dr. Gabel on my own computer. Both Missy and Shiloh loved the fact that I could work from home, and they soon got accustomed to my daily habits. Whenever I did go out, it was as a volunteer reading aide at the elementary school around the corner. I loved the expressions on the faces of the little ones as I read chapters from whatever book was chosen before I entered their classrooms. Somehow they always took me back to visualizing the faces of the children in Capri.

As I returned home from school one morning, I was met at my front door by the mailman. The envelope he handed me had numerous stamps on the front of the envelope, and the return address was Rome, Italy. I soon found myself standing inside my apartment, tearing open the envelope. One picture was inside. It was of a beautiful grove of trees with flowers everywhere. In the middle of the grove stood Angelo with his arms outstretched. On the back of the photograph was written: "New site for orphanage. God bless you!"

The anticipation of Dr. Gabel's portfolios always brought chills to my arms. Researching possible candidates to reward was gratifying, but flying off to confirm their deeds of human courage was the one and only act that made any sense to me. Whenever it arrived, wherever it took me, I knew I'd be ready to once again become his liaison with open arms *and* an open heart.

"Search for the joy in life. Hunt for it as for hidden treasure. Love and laugh. Delight yourselves in the Lord."

CPSIA information can be obtained at www.ICGtesting.com
Printed in the USA
LVOW081954030113

314104LV00003B/198/P